"Take your clothes off."

Kate's mouth curled up with a devilish twitch.

"Beg pardon?" He swallowed.

"You heard me, Ty. Strip. You trust me? Get your clothes off. Everything but your underwear."

Ty's eyes bored through the camera into hers. She felt it then, The Shift. Saw it in the way his muscles tensed. He licked his lips. "This is really what you want?"

"Getting there." Kate made her voice as smugly casual as she could, hoping the thick weight behind it would pass for boredom.

He unbuttoned and unzipped his pants and let them fall down his legs, revealing the powerful thighs that haunted Kate's dreams. Rock climber or not, Ty was built like a swimmer.

His body was long and lean, with cresting hip muscles that drew Kate's attention straight between his legs to the bulge in his boxer briefs. Lust banished Kate's misgivings and cemented her determination to see this through.

"How long have yo⬚⬚⬚⬚⬚⬚⬚ he asked, turning ⬚⬚⬚⬚⬚⬚

"From the very start

D1310974

Dear Reader,

Welcome to my very first Blaze novel! To say I'm flattered that you've picked up this book would be the understatement of a lifetime.

Though I've never been trapped in the snowy wilds of Saskatchewan with an Australian free climber (yet), I did throw myself fully into the research process for *Caught on Camera*. Much of that research consisted of forcing my then boyfriend, now husband, to watch hour upon hour of reality survival programs with me. That's hour upon hour of rather fit and capable men performing rugged acts of bravery, often shirtless.

Needless to say, it pained me greatly. Though neither of the hosts of my favorite shows were the basis for Ty's character, I offer my most heartfelt thanks for their suffering. Equally warm thanks go to the unseen masses behind the cameras and credits—I only hope Kate does your fascinating jobs a bit of justice.

And to my readers, thank you! If you have thoughts to share, please find me through my website www.megmaguire.com, blog or on Twitter. I'd love to hear your reactions to this, my first ever Blaze book.

Enjoy!

Meg Maguire

Meg Maguire

CAUGHT ON CAMERA

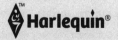

TORONTO NEW YORK LONDON
AMSTERDAM PARIS SYDNEY HAMBURG
STOCKHOLM ATHENS TOKYO MILAN MADRID
PRAGUE WARSAW BUDAPEST AUCKLAND

Recycling programs
for this product may
not exist in your area.

ISBN-13: 978-0-373-79612-0

CAUGHT ON CAMERA

Copyright © 2011 by Meghan Murphy

All rights reserved. Except for use in any review, the reproduction or utilization of this work in whole or in part in any form by any electronic, mechanical or other means, now known or hereafter invented, including xerography, photocopying and recording, or in any information storage or retrieval system, is forbidden without the written permission of the publisher, Harlequin Enterprises Limited, 225 Duncan Mill Road, Don Mills, Ontario M3B 3K9, Canada.

This is a work of fiction. Names, characters, places and incidents are either the product of the author's imagination or are used fictitiously, and any resemblance to actual persons, living or dead, business establishments, events or locales is entirely coincidental.

This edition published by arrangement with Harlequin Books S.A.

For questions and comments about the quality of this book please contact us at Customer_eCare@Harlequin.ca.

® and TM are trademarks of the publisher. Trademarks indicated with ® are registered in the United States Patent and Trademark Office, the Canadian Trade Marks Office and in other countries.

www.eHarlequin.com

Printed in U.S.A.

ABOUT THE AUTHOR

Before becoming a writer, Meg Maguire worked as a record store snob, a lousy barista, a decent designer and an overenthusiastic penguin handler. Now she loves writing sexy, character-driven stories about strong-willed men and women who keep each other on their toes…and bring one another to their knees. Meg lives north of Boston with her husband. When she's not trapped in her own head she can be found in the kitchen, the coffee shop or jogging around the nearest duck-filled pond.

To Amy and Jen,
who read it first and helped make it better.

To Laura and Brenda,
who recognized my voice behind all the profanity
and newbie mistakes, polished me up
and gave me a chance to shine.

To my parents and big brother, my extended family
and best friends, so supportive it's unnatural.

To the economy,
for taking away my day job
at the exact right moment.

And above all, thanks to my husband…
for putting up with me.
May all your ptarmigans be willowy.

1

KATE SCANNED THE TREES, one thought on her mind—food. *Food* being a very loose term. Roots, seeds, rodents, carrion…nearly anything would do in this desolate wasteland. In every direction, miles and miles of slushy spring snow, acres of scrubby pines, but lunch…?

"Fat frigging chance," she muttered. Then she saw it—a little clump of twigs in the crook of an old tree, a bird's nest. "Come on, eggs." Kate searched for handholds. She dug her boots into the knobby bark, locked her thighs around the trunk. Inch by slow, slippery inch, she made her clumsy ascent, mumbling a drum solo to herself. "Buh, buh-buh-buh-buh…" At moments like this, she always got the show's theme song stuck in her head.

Each episode opened with a flurry of bongos and a glimpse of misty green wilderness. Every few beats a new image flashed onto the screen—a man wading hip-deep through a rushing river, scaling a sheer cliff face, striking a flint. Words burst onto the screen—*Dom Tyler: Survive This!* The title disappeared to make way for a second bout of montage overlaid with credits that went ignored by most viewers in favor of the handsome man with his dirty blond hair and fascinating eyes, arms like a boxer and smile like a natural-born con man.

Kate knew the show's opening by heart. Heck, she'd filmed half the footage herself. And she knew Dom Tyler by heart, too. Those arms and that smile belonged to her boss, her best friend. And it was his fault she was halfway up a tree in the desolate wilds of Saskatchewan just now, wrecking her jeans with sap.

Wincing at the bark digging into her thighs, she took a deep breath and hauled herself onto a thick branch, ten feet off the ground. Bingo—eggs.

"Woo hoo!" She pumped her fist in the air. Glancing toward the campsite, she bellowed, "Ty! I've found your lunch!"

A faint noise of acknowledgment drifted through the otherwise silent landscape. Balancing on the limb, Kate slid the video camera strapped across her back forward and shouldered it. She aimed the viewfinder at the three ill-fated eggs nestled in the wreath of twigs and hit the record button.

"Songbird eggs," she murmured into the mic. "Need a confirm on the species. Early spring is one of the best times of year to find bird eggs if you get lost in the Canadian wilderness—double-check that fact. They can be cooked, or eaten raw if fire is scarce, and they're a great source of protein."

The show was an hour long, forty-two minutes after commercials. Forty-two minutes of Dom Tyler explaining how to stay alive in some of the world's harshest environments—a different location each episode. Though his looks likely distracted most viewers from actually retaining any of the lessons.

For nearly every shot that made it to air, just off camera stood Kate, armed with the stern poise of a lion tamer and a hastily acquired vocabulary to rival David Attenborough's. She researched and wrote nearly half of the show's narration. It was Dom Tyler's name in the title and face on the screen, but she was the one behind him, cracking the whip, keeping the show and its host on track.

She let the camera roll a few more seconds before shouldering it and fumbling back down the trunk, hopping the last few feet to the soggy ground.

"Ty?" Ty, because he winced whenever anyone called him Dominic. Kate headed toward the fire they'd set up by the river, shouting to him as she picked pine needles from the front of her jacket. "We're going to need to get you up there. I want some climbing and hand shots. I made some notes you can record in postproduction."

She rounded the bend at the edge of the woods and discovered why Ty wasn't shouting back. Sitting splay-legged on a fallen tree, he had one of the other cameras perched on his broad shoulder, its lens trained on Kate, red light blinking. As she neared, she heard him narrating for his own amusement, a raised whisper in the Australian accent that earned them at least a quarter of their ratings.

"…the natural habitat of the Kate Somersby. We can see from her stance that this approach is one of postured aggression, though the look in the female's eyes suggests that mating may be on her mind. Let's wait and see what she's after." Ty abandoned the voice-over as Kate pushed her boot against the front of his vest, toppling him harmlessly backward into the wet snow.

She crossed her arms over her chest and mustered her best fed-up assistant glare. It was day two of their three-day exile in this snowy wasteland, and cold was not her strong suit. "Some of us have been scaling trees, Ty. Earning our saddle sores."

"That's one way to get your rocks off."

"I need you up there." She stared down at her professional partner of the past two and a half years, blatantly appraising all six feet three inches of him, from his boot-clad feet up to his unruly golden-brown hair and sideburns, and that evil, evil eyebrow. His chin and jaw were peppered with several days' blond stubble. By the time they got back to L.A. he'd probably have a full-on beard. It wouldn't do a thing to disguise his movie-star good looks, just as his clothes couldn't trick their viewers into forgetting what was hidden beneath, once they'd caught a glimpse.

Kate knew what lay beneath the thermal shirt Ty currently wore under his vest, too. She knew it with more familiarity than she'd known the body of any former lover, despite the fact that she and Ty had never so much as kissed. That disappointed certain parts of her, relieved others. She loved her job too much to risk it over something as stupid as hormones. And she loved Ty, too—as a friend. She wouldn't risk losing *him*, either…though the thought of such a mistake had certainly kept her warm on a few cold nights.

She gave Ty's hovering foot a soft kick. "C'mon, up you get. Eggs."

Ty groaned. "God, eggs."

"Tell me about it." She grabbed the hand he stuck out and yanked him up to sitting. "I've got a few of my own that'll be going to waste in a few years, if I keep running around the globe with the likes of you."

"So you keep telling me…but don't pretend you don't love this." He wiped wet snow off the backs of his arms, zipped the camera into its sturdy bag and set it aside.

Kate sat down beside him on a log. He was right, of course. For all its ridiculous moments, she adored this job. And not just the job—but their partnership. Plus she was an unapologetic control freak and this gig allowed her to do what she did best on a grand scale, and get paid for it. At twenty-eight, thoughts of settling into a normal life could wait a few more years, or as long as the network continued to renew their contract.

Ty took her handheld camera and reviewed the footage, frowning. "Why is it you never find us wild rib-eye?"

"Why is it you never find us anything, period?" she asked, though it was a mean exaggeration. Ty more than pulled his weight, but today he was noticeably unfocused. Kate wasn't surprised. He was running on very little food and even less sleep.

He handed the camera back and stared at her with the unearthly blue-green eyes that earned them another quarter of their ratings.

"What?"

"Nothing." His tone suggested otherwise. "Take me to your eggs."

"Terrifying choice of words, Ty." They stood and she tossed him the wool hat he'd been wearing in the previous scene. He tugged it on and followed her back to the tree.

"Third limb."

He squinted upward. "I see it."

She trained the camera on Ty as he demonstrated how to loop a length of climbing rope around the trunk to make the task easier. Kate frowned at her ruined jeans and savaged thighs. In three minutes he was up and back again with the eggs in his vest pocket.

"What d'you fancy?" he asked, his perpetually mischievous eyebrow cocked at her. "Raw or boiled?"

"It's your lunch, Ty. I'm having an energy bar."

"What'll look better?" he asked.

"You cooked that goose, yesterday. Better do an 'if you can't build a fire' scenario."

"You're the boss."

She pursed her lips, skeptical. "Care to put that in writing?"

Ty merely smirked, a dimple forming beside one corner of his mouth. Technically speaking, of course, he was the boss. It wasn't just his name on the show, either—in addition to being the host and narrator of the wildly popular reality program, he was also its creator. He'd dreamed it up, pitched it, got himself the contract and come to the table with much of his survival experience already hard-earned from a stint in his twenties as a globe-trekking rock climber.

"How are we getting to tomorrow's location?" Ty asked as he set up a tripod for the raw-egg-eating shot.

"Do you even look at the itineraries I write up for you?"

He angled the lens, fiddled with the settings. "Don't need to, Katie. I've got you."

"May God have mercy on the woman you trick into marrying you one day, Ty." *Not that you're the marrying kind,* she added to herself. She pulled her copy of the meticulous memorandum from the back pocket of her filthy jeans. "We're meeting the dogsled folks tomorrow morning at five. The trip should take about three hours, then we're doing an ice-fishing spot if the lake up there's still frozen. Snowmobile team's picking us up at sundown."

"Beautiful. And after tomorrow?"

Kate smiled at the thought. "You know."

Ty met her eyes above the camera. "Tell me anyhow, Katie. I love to hear you say it."

"After tomorrow, we're done for another season."

Ty sighed, loud and dramatic. "And so our next destination will be…?"

"I don't know about you, but mine'll be my bed." She could practically feel her cool sheets and soft pillows now.

"Sounds good. I'll see you there."

Kate waited until Ty glanced at her before she fixed him with a look she hoped conveyed her grumpy exhaustion. "While we're on the topic, may I make a suggestion or two, for next season's locales?"

"Mmm?"

"I'm thinking Maui. Saint John's? Fiji? Please? This snow is killing me."

"You're from New England," he said, eyes swiveling back to the camera's screen.

"And I hated snow growing up, too. Come on, Ty...lost at sea? Even that's got to be better than this."

He shook his head. "No open ocean stuff."

"Why are you so weird about—"

"I get seasick," Ty interrupted. "Quiet on the set."

He switched the camera on and went to work. Kate fell silent, smirking to herself. Only Dom Tyler could make swallowing the contents of raw songbird eggs erotic. Unlikely as it seemed, this shot was pure gold when it came to capturing the viewers' attention. And with the snowy locale, this episode needed all the help it could get. Even though it was technically spring, winter still felt very much like the order of the day here in Saskatchewan. Winter meant snow and ice, gusting winds and cruel cold. And layers. Layers made the chance that the viewers would get a glimpse of Ty's bare torso seem less likely. And that meant fewer pairs of anticipating eyes glued to the screen—the top half of Ty's body secured them the largest chunk of their enviable viewership. They were by far the best-performing show on their nature- and travel-based network, and survival had very little to do with it.

"The viewers are going to love that," Kate said when he finished recording.

"Our viewers are kinky, then...present company included." He smiled at her, dismantling the tripod.

Kate bit back a smile of her own. "I'm immune to your charms, thank you very much. And if the viewers had to spend as much time with you as I do, they'd feel the same way."

Ty faked offense, raising his eyebrows. "Now don't tell me this isn't what you were expecting when you moved to L.A. I mean, tell me *this* isn't Hollywood glitz and glamour at its best." He waved an arm around, indicating the dreary landscape, the minimalist campsite and the two of them. He hadn't bathed since they'd left Los Angeles three days earlier, the antithesis of glamour. Kate wasn't looking much better.

"I never thought being a personal assistant would be glamorous."

"Of course not." He grinned at her, looking skeptical. "Your coffee table's only covered in celebrity mags because you couldn't find any coasters, I'm sure."

Kate pushed the slushy snow around with her foot. "Being a PA—the kind I thought I'd be," she corrected, "is pretty slummy. I assumed I'd be fetching twelve-dollar lattes, and wiping poodle crap off somebody's stilettos. Holding some celebutante's hair back while she puked discreetly in the alley behind the poshest club in Hollywood. That sort of thing."

"Very classy," Ty said. "But I know there's more. Don't think I can't see you salivating when the swag turns up."

True. They'd been making this show for three seasons now and Ty was beginning to qualify as a bona fide TV celebrity. Kate had nearly hyperventilated the first time a designer offered Ty a suit to wear to an awards ceremony. He'd ultimately blown the event off in favor of a Lakers game and she'd grudgingly returned the goods.

"This isn't exactly what I'd pictured…more frostbite, fewer flashbulbs. And you aren't exactly the boss I'd pictured, either," she admitted, squinting at him as they walked back to the fire. "I'd imagined a starlet with a diet-pill habit, not some nature-boy with an adrenaline addiction. And this isn't the skill set I thought I'd be gaining."

Ty dragged a frame pack over and extracted a length of rope from the front pocket, tossing it to Kate. "Bowline," he ordered in his best drill sergeant's voice.

Kate made a perfect bowline knot in seconds flat. One of a hundred talents she'd learned from Ty and from books since landing this crazy job.

"Double figure eight."

She tied a beauty.

"I bet Reese Witherspoon's PA can't do that," Ty said smugly.

"No, and I bet she can't treat a snakebite or diagnose dengue fever." Kate made a loose slipknot and tossed it around his neck. "Now that I think about it, Ty, this gig's not really teaching me any of the skills I'll need if I'm going to run a powerful Hollywood agency someday. I thought I'd be reading *Variety* in first class, not manuals about ice-cave exploration in the back of a Cessna."

He shrugged. "Funny what choices the universe makes for you."

"Yeah. My cosmic dart didn't land quite where I'd expected," Kate added, referring to Ty's new preferred method of choosing their shoot locations—tossing a dart blindly at a world map until it hit an appropriately forbidding destination. He had a penchant for leaving decisions up to chance, an aversion to caution that bordered on superstition.

He slid a long hunting knife from the sheath on his belt and slapped the handle into Kate's palm. He pointed to a spruce tree a few yards away and stepped back.

Kate took aim and threw. The knife whipped through

the air and the blade found its target, thwacking into the trunk, dead center.

Ty groaned and clapped a hand over his heart as if he were fighting an arousal-induced heart attack. "Goddamn, woman."

Kate smiled to herself, and hoped the cold breeze would banish the prideful flush warming her cheeks.

Ty slipped the rope from his head and put it away. "And to think, when I met you you'd never even had poison ivy before."

"That's not true."

"Well, you had a manicure. You can't deny that. What have I done to you?"

"Nothing I didn't ask for," Kate said, rising to the flirtation. True, this show was most definitely not the job she'd envisioned when she'd started looking for work as an assistant, fresh off the plane from the East Coast. She'd been desperate and had no experience, and Ty had simply been the first person who'd succumbed to her strong-arming and hired her. Unlikely or not, it had evolved into Kate's dream job. The travel and new experiences comprised a part of that, but secretly, the real appeal was Ty himself. Kate looked him over again, eyeballing the man who'd easily become her best friend these past couple years. The closest friend she'd ever had…though she'd never told him as much. She took a seat on the log, stretching her achy legs out in front of her.

"You may not be grooming me for a gig as an agent," Kate said, "but I'll settle for executive producer."

"You're practically that already." Ty jogged to the tree and retrieved his knife, slid it into its sheath as he trudged back. "I know you thought you'd be choosing my thousand-dollar wristwatches instead of pulling leeches off me, but no one can deny you're still an ace at running my life."

Kate smiled with indulgence. "And that's exactly what I wanted."

"Control freak."

"Death wish," she shot back. "And like it or not, you'll be in *GQ* before you know it. The glamour will follow," she murmured, dreamy, holding her hands out as if envisioning their future rendezvous with stylists and PR agencies.

"So you say."

"Plus this gig is a fantastic workout." She flexed her arm. Her figure had certainly benefited from two-plus years of this demanding lifestyle. "And my passport's got an enviable collection of stamps."

"Good to know there are some positive side effects to putting up with me," he said. "And you're always up to the challenge."

"I survived three nights in Death Valley, Ty. I think I can handle the likes of you."

Kate wrapped up their banter with an emphatic slap of her hands on her thighs and stood, refocusing on the task at hand. She grabbed a half-frozen protein bar out of her pack, gnawing on it while Ty stowed the tripod.

"How do we get your shirt off in this episode?" she asked, chewing.

"I'm thinking sweat, hypothermia danger, drying clothes by the fire?"

She frowned. "We do that in like, every single snow scenario."

"Yeah, and it's the most legit rationale." He let slip a hint of rare irritation. "But I'm listening. What's your brilliant idea this time?"

"You want to fall in an icy river?"

He finished tidying the campsite and stared at her, arms locked over his chest. "I don't, but I'll bet it's top of your list."

"Use your shirt to rig a makeshift fishing net?"

"Better." He took a couple steps closer.

"Torn off by a cougar in a fight to the death?"

He stopped right in front of her. "You're way too young to qualify as a cougar, Katie."

"Cute," she drawled disapprovingly, but The Shift had already happened. That's how Kate described it to herself, this change as Ty went into his shameless playboy shtick. To him this flirtation was a game, a distraction she was certain he only orchestrated to get on her nerves. But its effects ran deeper than she'd ever let him know. Ten thousand women probably had school-girl crushes on Dom Tyler, and Kate didn't need him knowing she was among them. Still, when he got that gleam in his eye and lowered his voice to that devious hush, he was more than just Kate's friend and boss. He was the man who set her on fire off camera, no flint or tinder required.

"We need at least another couple hours of footage today," she said, easing the zipper of his vest halfway down his front. "So get that look out of your eye." She jerked the zipper back up to his stubbly chin and gave his cheek a couple of light slaps.

"Taskmaster."

She sighed. "Somebody has to be."

Still mired deep in The Shift, Ty ran his hands up and over Kate's shoulders, his calloused thumbs pressing the pulse points of her jugular, as they always did at this moment. A moment that been taunting Kate continually for the past two years and then some. God, two years…

His smirking mouth inched closer as he stooped to eclipse the considerable difference in their heights. The weather-roughened skin of his lips grazed her temple, her cheek, her jaw. His lips neared hers until their noses touched, and then he smiled. This was the point when he always smiled.

"Oh," he said, pantomime realization furrowing his brow and dampening the growl in his voice.

"What?" Kate prompted, her refrain weary.

He sighed with theatrical regret. "Forgot I just ate those raw eggs."

"Yes, of course." She rolled her eyes.

Ty withdrew, just as he'd done in exactly this same fashion a hundred times before. "Can't risk giving you salmonella."

"No, obviously not." But Kate wouldn't mind giving him blue balls. Was there a female equivalent? If so, she'd had a clinically dangerous case for a long time now.

The first time he'd done that, when they'd been filming the first season's final episode, she'd fallen for it. That mouth, sliding down past her good ear, those fingers on her throat—hook, line and sinker. Close enough to feel his breath heating her cheek, and then, "Katie?"

And then her breathless, "Yes?"

And then, "I've just remembered. We haven't checked our shoes for scorpions. One of the leading causes of avoidable tragedy in the desert."

Infuriating. Who flirted like that? Week after week after week? A stunning Australian sociopath with a risk predilection, apparently.

Before the show had come about, Ty had been a fringe celebrity in Australia and in certain sporting circles. He'd gone to school in Sydney for filmmaking then spent several years as a quasi-professional free climber. He was a bit of an anomaly—or a moron, as some asserted—as he'd climbed in remote areas, without a partner or any safety precautions. He'd taped himself as he was climbing, much like the show, one camera capturing the scene, the other recording from his own vantage point as he dangled from cliff faces. Kate had tracked down a bunch of those videos back when she'd been looking into this job. Watching them, she'd known some of what she was getting herself into, dangerwise. Attractionwise she'd been woefully unprepared. Her less professional feelings for Ty had trickled in slowly, grown as their friendship did and as their joint project gained success. Those feelings had eventually snowballed into a full-blown infatuation, but potent or not they were nothing compared to Kate's fear of rejection. She'd been left by enough people already...her father when she was tiny, her fiancé at twenty-five. Plus her mother, who'd technically always been around, but had never really ever *been* there. History had taught Kate that whenever she let herself grow attached to somebody, they ditched her, and she'd left that pattern behind her, along with the rest of her crappy former life on the outskirts of Boston.

Here in the present, Ty flashed her a merciless smile, his eyes lit up in the cold northern sunlight. "God, that was a close one."

She rolled her eyes again—like hell it was. This exchange was like clockwork in its methodology. Water torture. Drop by drop, month after month. No small wonder Kate sometimes felt as if she were drowning.

"You are so unprofessional," she sighed. Silly as it was, this little routine always left Kate feeling vulnerable. She tugged reflexively on her bad ear. It still ached sometimes, even twenty-plus years after she'd recovered from the infection that had taken most of her hearing on that side. She kept her eyes trained on the ground, hoping once again that her face wasn't coloring. Her good mood waned. In its wake she shivered, remembering how tired and cold she was.

"I'm going to get some panoramas," she grumbled, meaning the sweeping scenery shots they used to fill the air between action sequences. The film editors spliced them in and the music guy added appropriately grand- or dire-sounding accompaniment for whatever the location was. She suspected most of their female viewers simply tolerated these scenes, impatient for the next shot of Ty.

Kate walked a short distance and began recording. In the finished product they tried to give the illusion that Ty did all the work himself, but anyone with half a brain knew the unsteady camera that was frequently filming him had a person behind it. A disclaimer flashed on the screen just after the show's opening sequence, designed to render this masquerade acceptable. *Do not attempt these survival scenarios. Dom Tyler has a trained crew assisting him. This program is for entertainment only.*

Boots crunched on the snow behind Kate to give away her partner's approach. Even if they hadn't, she could sense him. Ty had an energy that made everything near him vibrate at the same frequency. Kate liked that about him. It gave her a contact high, a taste of the chaos she worked so hard to keep at bay in her own body and brain.

She kept her eyes on the camera. "What is it, Ty?"

"What are you going to have for dinner tonight when we get back to town?" he asked from just behind her right shoulder.

She shook her head. "Masochist." Ty never ate what he couldn't hunt or scavenge from the wild when they were in the middle of making an episode.

"You going to have a beer?" he asked.

She didn't reply.

"You going to have six beers and finally make a pass at me?"

"Doubtful, Ty. I'd need about a fifth of whiskey and a handsome bribe for that to happen."

"My PA could arrange that."

"Oh, *could* she?" Kate turned to fix him with her best impression of an unamused assistant.

Ty commenced to sing, shamelessly. It was a song off an old cassette by the Puerto Rican boy band Menudo. Though neither Kate nor Ty spoke Spanish beyond the tourist level, she suspected a native speaker would find his rendition damn near fluent—they'd listened to that tape a hell of a lot.

"Doesn't it take you back, Kate?" Ty asked, interrupting his own vocals. "What was your favorite Torture Tape?"

"As the driver, or the passenger?"

"Driver," Ty said.

One of Kate's very first assignments as Ty's PA was to find them a vehicle big enough to transport the filming and camping gear and safe enough to get them from Honduras to Alaska—since their initial budget hadn't allowed for air travel—and cheap enough to make Kate's eyes roll at the ridiculousness of the task. When they were on the road in that ancient death trap, whoever got stuck driving was allowed to torture the passenger by playing the most obnoxious secondhand cassette they could find, ad nauseum.

Kate pondered the question before lowering her eye to the viewfinder once more. "I thought the soundtrack to *The Little Mermaid* was one of my better efforts."

"That *was* pretty rough…although I prefer it over Mariah Carey. At least the way you sing it."

Kate made herself sound more exasperated than she was. "Can I help you with something, Ty?"

"Don't you miss the van? I do."

She sighed. "I don't know what I miss the most…the Naugahyde ripping the skin off the backs of my thighs in the Mexican heat, the leak above the passenger seat. The way it broke down every five thousand miles so we had to sleep in the back."

"Don't forget the mysterious latex smell," Ty added.

"It'll still be there when we get back to L.A. For now I'm

actually enjoying having a vehicle with a working radio for a change."

"Well, not me." Ty fell silent a few moments as Kate resumed filming, then she felt him toying with her short ponytail. "You fancy a snowball fight?" he asked. "I'll give you first throw."

"Please go back to work, Ty. Get me twenty more minutes of commentary. We need to pack up in an hour, anyhow. Do your MacGyver challenge."

He gave her ponytail a final flick before he left her, tromping back toward the campsite, belting out Los Lobos. She shook her head. It was like herding toddlers some days, though to be fair, once the work was done, she was just as bad. All the time she'd spent traveling with Ty had brought out facets of her personality she hadn't even known were there. He saw her at her stinkiest and bitchiest and least lovable, and he still stuck around, totally unfazed. It was the closest thing to unconditional love she'd ever known.

A few minutes later Kate clicked the camera off and headed back to camp to find Ty crouching a few paces from a tripod, addressing the mic. She checked to make sure her shadow wasn't about to creep into his shot then tiptoed around him to get to her pack. He was good. When the camera was on, Ty could ignore her presence like she wasn't even there.

"…and ptarmigans and some larger rodents, although as you've noticed, I haven't been so lucky. Let's pretend I was, though, for the sake of storytelling—let me show you another way to make a fire. We've got some decent sun right now, so I want to try something with that disposable camera the crew included in my little arsenal." He abandoned the shot to gather a few things, returning to show their future audience how to smash up a cheap point-and-click to get the lens out and use it to ignite the cardboard housing.

Kate walked over as he wrapped the segment. "Very nice. See how fun it is to do your job?"

"Thanks for the disposable."

"That was an easy one," she said. "Your MacGyver rating was only about a three."

"You ought to be challenging me a bit more, then. Time to head to town?"

Kate consulted her waterproof watch. "Yeah. Let's get packed up."

The snowmobile team would arrive in short order to bring them back to the one-traffic-light-town they'd based the expedition in. They'd drop their stuff off at the motor court and go in search of dinner, and in just a few short hours the other Ty would come knocking. The thought made Kate shiver inside her more-than-adequately-warm coat.

2

"AH, CIVILIZATION." Ty slid onto a bar stool beside Kate, relieved for a bit of padding under his frozen, beaten body. He sat on her right as always. She'd never told him exactly what had happened to her left ear, but he didn't pry. Getting questioned about her childhood snapped Kate up tighter than a bear trap…and besides, Ty didn't particularly fancy returning the favor. Secrets didn't bother him. What he had with Kate was better. They lived in the present and took each other at face value.

He studied her in the red-and-blue glow of the beer signs and settled into the warmth, as easily as he settled into his friend's company. He loved that about Kate—the comfort. Ty hadn't felt that with anyone else, not girlfriends or drinking buddies or old college mates, not even his family, at least not since he'd been very young. But with Kate…effortless. Set loose in the current of their no-frills rapport, Ty was able to let go and simply drift.

She ordered a pint and a cheeseburger and Ty waved politely but dismissively at the bartender. He watched Kate grab some napkins, already preparing for her feast. Then Ty nudged her shoulder with his. "God, you're mean."

She turned to him, resting her elbow on the shiny wooden

bar and her chin in her hand. "It's your rule, Ty. No one told you you're not allowed to eat."

He shifted on his stool, trying to twist some of the achiness from his muscles. Saskatchewan was cold and damp and its early darkness made him miss Australia with a rare but tangible pang. Or maybe that was just his empty stomach. He looked at Kate. "Well, you'd think you might want to join me, you know, out of solidarity. Just once."

"Don't hold your breath, boss."

"You know my idea for when we run out of places to film in the wild?" he asked, spinning a coaster around on the bar.

Her eyebrow rose. "That thing where you pose as a homeless person and survive for a week on the streets of Detroit?"

He shrugged. "Or Delhi, or Lagos. What d'you reckon? It's sounding pretty good right now. At least I could go to a soup kitchen." He picked up the coaster and balanced it on Kate's head.

She gave a contemptuous snort. "Nobody's going to fall for you as a homeless person." She took the coaster off her head and poked his upper arm with it. "Not with triceps like those. And you can't do an American accent to save your life. You sound like a South African Rocky Balboa."

"I could get a voice coach."

She shook her head. "No way."

"What about my other idea, then? 'Dom Tyler: Undercover in San Quentin. Survive This, Law-Abider!' Prison food's sounding pretty good right about now. Showers."

"And shivs and gang wars and dropped soap? Forget it."

The barman delivered Kate's beer. She drew it close, sucking the foam off the top before picking up the glass, gazing over the rim at Ty with indulgent cruelty. Maybe it was his own maddening hunger, but every time she did that Ty couldn't help but imagine it was the sort of look she'd give a man right after she tossed the handcuff keys all the way across the room.

She groaned with obscene satisfaction. "Damn, that's good."

"I'll bet." Ty offered her a smile that said he wasn't finding her the least bit cute. And that was sort of true. She wasn't cute. She was dead sexy.

Ty squinted at her as her French fries arrived. People called Kate cute all the time. She was petite, with the clearest, most luminous skin Ty had ever seen, like a face wash model. And shoulder-length dark brown hair, straighter and shinier than even a shampoo ad would dare to promise. Sure, she looked cute. Much the way a rabid kitten might seem adorable, right up until you made the mistake of petting it.

"What are you staring at, Ty? Do I have ketchup on my face?" She wiped a thumb over the corners of her mouth.

Cute… Ty knew better. He saw Kate when no one else was around, at all hours of the day and night, at her best and her worst. In dresses and heels at cocktail parties and in his own boxers and undershirt while her filthy clothes were drying by a bonfire in some godforsaken stretch of remote wilderness. *Sexy.* Sexy when she chased him down to exact her revenge for a well-aimed snowball to the face, sexy when she greeted him half-asleep, grudging smile framed behind the chain-lock of her motel room door at 3 a.m.

Kate's burger arrived and she luxuriated in it, a cat in a sunbeam.

"I hate you," Ty murmured, mouth watering for more than just the burger.

"Oh man, this is amazing. So juicy."

"I hope you get food poisoning."

"I suppose I'm overdue," she said through a bite.

That was true enough. The number of times she'd smoothed Ty's hair off his forehead and rubbed his back while he suffered through the consequences of an ill-advised meal out in the woods… She'd said she was prepared to do anything as a PA, no matter how unglitzy, but she couldn't have meant all this. One day she was going to reach her limit, and though it'd kill Ty to lose her, at least he'd finally be able to make good on those threats his body issued whenever he came within two breaths of kissing her. Such as now, for instance.

"Do you want my pickle?" she asked with sickly sweet innocence. "I could toss it out into the snow. That wouldn't be cheating. You'd still technically be foraging."

"I'm going to break into your room when you're showering and flush the toilet on you."

She grinned, eyes narrowing. "Maybe I should order dessert," she whispered, and took another bite.

"Evil." Evil for more than this food flaunting—for flirting back when Ty knew she'd never go there with him as long as they were professional partners. Kate put her job above everything, surely far above any attraction she might feel for him. If they ever got their moment, it'd have to come after the show was canceled. On especially long nights, when he and Kate were the only humans for miles around and he lay awake listening to her steady breathing in a dark tent or the back of the van, Ty prayed for bad ratings.

"What would you have right now, if you could, Ty?" Kate's eyes darted to the chalkboard menu behind the bar. "Steak?" she guessed, perusing the fare. "Fried chicken and mashed potatoes?"

He offered his best Sean-Connery-as-Bond accent. "Don't toy with me, Moneypenny."

"Something not on the menu?" Kate asked with raised

eyebrows, a distinct challenge. Get a drink or two in this girl and she turned into a flirting machine.

Ty rose to the dare she was posing, licking his lips. "Such as...?"

She leaned in closer, fixing her eyes on his. "I know exactly what you want," she said. She was only teasing, but Ty's body responded nonetheless.

"What do I want, Katie?"

"Ooh, I'm thinking...crab," she concluded. "Legs. With lots of melted butter and new potatoes." She did know what he liked. She knew him better than she probably even realized, and that's what made Ty's attraction tougher and tougher to write off the longer they worked together. She gave a last wiggle of her eyebrows before she sat up straight again.

"I could fire you, you know."

"Yeah right, Ty. You'd be lost without me." She turned to watch the television mounted in the corner. A newscaster was droning about a late-season storm warning, but Ty thought Kate ought to be more concerned with the imminent threat her flirtation was causing. He watched her expression change as she turned to him again.

"You know, you and I are like *every*thing except lovers," she said.

The statement threw Ty for a momentary loop. Hope and lust jockeyed for his attention, warming him like whiskey, from the inside. "Yeah. Why? You looking to change that?"

She smirked at his tone, shook her head and took another sip of beer. "Nope."

Ty's body cooled with disappointment. "Why not?"

"Well, mainly because it's the worst idea I've ever heard."

Ty rolled his eyes. "Brilliant. Thanks for even bringing it up, then."

"But I was just thinking how it's interesting, about you and me." She wagged a French fry between them. "I mean, we've managed to make all this work for three whole seasons now, under the most stressful conditions possible. But we're both still totally useless with relationships."

"Oh, cheers. And wait—so, indulge my fragile male ego a moment, but why's it such a rubbish idea, exactly?"

"Because if, no, *when* we screwed it all up, we'd both have nothing," she said. "And I spent a lo-o-ong time having nothing, and it sucks. I don't plan on going back to it. And definitely not over sex."

"We've survived tropical storms and quicksand and network mergers together," Ty said. "You don't think we could survive maybe drinking a bit too much and waking up next to each other?"

"Not a chance I'm willing to take, Ty. Plus I wake up next to you all the time and trust me, it's grossly overrated."

He put a hand to his chest, faking a blow to his heart. "You are stone-cold, Katie."

She shrugged, eyes drifting to the TV above the bar. "It's Saskatchewan."

Ty leaned into the bar, mirroring her body. He made sure he kept the flirtation over-the-top, joking, always their way. "What if it was *really* good sex?"

Kate smirked and shook her head again.

"You don't know what we might be missing out on."

"I'll live. And anyhow, I'd get strung up by tall women everywhere for poaching in their rightful territory."

Ty switched tracks. "What if we weren't all those other things? What if the show got canceled tomorrow?"

He saw thoughts forming, gears ticking behind Kate's unfocused eyes as she chose what bones to throw him, picked whether to tease him or pull him up short. In the end she did both. "I dunno, Ty. And I don't intend to find out… But if that day does ever come, and we can still stand the sight of each other, you have permission to make a pass at me—a real one. But not a moment before."

She sat up straight and aimed her attention back at her food. Ten minutes later she slid her half-full second glass of beer back across the counter. Ty watched the barman take it away as if it were his firstborn being wrenched from his arms. Damn, he'd kill for a beer right about now. He let that craving replace the one that had taken up residence between his thighs.

"Bedtime," Kate said with a satisfied yawn—a postcoital yawn if ever he'd heard one.

They walked side by side back to the motor court, hugging their bodies against the bone-deep cold. They mounted the outside steps to the second level of rooms and bid one another good-night under the yellow glow of the parking lot's lights. Ty watched Kate's softly swishing hips carry her a few paces to her door, watched her find her key and disappear into her room with a final smile over her shoulder.

He'd be good tonight. He was tired. He could make it—what, six hours? Ty searched his pockets for his own key and heard Kate's dead bolt click. He knew already he'd hear it again before long, sliding back open to let him in. Who was he trying to kid, anyhow?

WHEN THE INEVITABLE KNOCK came at her door, Kate rolled over to groggily scan the digital screen of her trusty travel alarm clock. Three twenty-eight…dear God in Heaven. Already knowing what this would be about, she resigned herself to leaving the warm cocoon of the sheets and shuffled to the door.

She squinted into the jaundiced light. "Morning, Ty."

A frigid breeze seeped in behind him. "Invite me in?"

"Yup. Knock yourself out."

Kate had long ago learned that having a handsome, strapping man with an exotic accent turn up on her doorstep in the dead of night didn't necessary mean what one might hope. She'd also learned to sleep with a bra on if Ty was staying in the same motel as her. It just saved a lot of time and modesty not having to scramble for one night after night.

As her guest strolled past in track pants and a bawdy T-shirt he'd purchased with her in Tijuana, Kate flipped the television on. She checked their channel's Canadian sister just in case their show was on in reruns, but it was mired in infomercials. She heard Ty's flip-flops land on the carpet and the rustling of the sheets as he made a space for himself on her bed. Those sounds shouldn't still give her a charge after all this time, but they always did. And actually, why shouldn't they? Everything she'd said in the bar still stood—she wouldn't ever complicate what they had by throwing sex into the mix. But that didn't mean she couldn't think about it.

She sat on the edge of the bed, setting the remote by Ty's elbow. He stretched out on his stomach, facing the screen, and Kate ran her hands through his messy hair, trying to establish some kind of order. This was allowed, another extension of their nearly all-encompassing whatevership, but God knew why. Unspoken understanding allowed them to do a lot of things that they both knew they'd better knock off if one of them started seeing someone else. Not inherently incriminating things, but ones no significant other could ever reasonably be expected to put up with.

She sighed. "You couldn't wait another hour, Ty?"

"Can't sleep over there. There's a rattle in the heating vent or something."

"Sure there is."

He always had an excuse for turning up. Ty was a terrible sleeper, practically an insomniac, but Kate didn't fully understand her own role in these predictable intrusions. Experience had taught her that Ty was useless at any activity that required him to remain still for longer than thirty seconds, but why keeping her awake seemed to cure his sleeping disorder remained an inconvenient mystery.

He groaned happily, settling in. That sound… It brought back memories Kate could have done without. It had been two years now since she'd accidentally walked in on him having sex with his then-girlfriend, but the images of it were clear as day. Blissfully, Ty was still none the wiser.

Back in L.A., Ty lived in an apartment Kate had found for him after the first season wrapped, one far more to her taste than his. She suspected he'd be happy in some craphole studio by the freeway, but she'd snagged him what she felt an up-and-coming TV personality should have. He'd hated the wall-to-wall carpeting on sight, but to this day Kate said a little thank-you prayer whenever she laid eyes on it.

She'd had keys to his place and had gotten in the habit of coming by unannounced to go over rough cuts of the show or to drop off papers for him. She'd since gotten out of this habit.

When she came by that traumatic evening she'd let herself in as usual and followed the sounds of the television to Ty's living room, just as she'd done a dozen times before. The hall light had been off and the maligned carpeting hadn't given away her footsteps, so by the time she reached the threshold she'd given the two preoccupied bodies on the couch no reason to halt their happy activities. For a half a minute Kate had stood there, frozen.

From across the room she'd watched the long expanse of Ty's bare back, elegant muscles writhing, his sculpted ass and hips pumping hard, flanked on either side by two svelte, female legs. Kate had smelled it, too, that raw, hot, sex smell. She'd heard Ty over the murmur of the TV, his animal moans and grunts blending with the woman's. Kate had slunk back out of the apartment unnoticed. Her blood ran hot at the memory, the sight of another woman's hands on Ty's bare body.

He spoke, snapping Kate from her trance. "What are you thinking about?"

She blinked, felt a blush warm her face and thanked God it was dark. "Do you remember Angie?"

"Of course. I dated her for almost a month. That's like a record."

"I was thinking about her," Kate said, casual. *Thinking about her freakishly long legs wrapped around your waist.* "I don't get why you two broke up. She was like the female equivalent of you."

"That should be your reason, right there."

"She seemed nice enough," Kate offered, feeling him out.

"She was lovely," he confirmed. "I think she's a hosiery model now. Bit of a waste…she was a smart one, dating choices aside."

Kate had been out to dinner with the pair of them a few times and was always left feeling like Ty's kid sister. If a tigress like Angie couldn't keep Ty occupied then a comparable mouse like Kate was dead in the water. Not that she was looking to, of course. Definitely not.

"But Angie was odd, too," Ty offered, making Kate's dangerous train of thought jump its tracks. "She had that daft little yappy dog. And she paid to have her *eyelashes* dyed. What is it with L.A. women?" He yawned and settled them on a channel rebroadcasting a trashy talk show. Folding his arms under his chin, Ty got comfortable, setting the remote by Kate's leg.

"You've only got about forty minutes before we need to be up and presentable," she reminded him.

"I'll take it."

Kate offered another sigh, long and melodramatic. "You're so weird."

Ty could usually manage about three or four hours on his own during these trips before he crawled into Kate's bed, demanding distraction or soothing. He transformed into a different man at night. Restless and moody and needy, so different from his on-camera self, that picture of confidence and charisma. Kate read in his body what he needed from her. She circled her palm between his shoulder blades.

"Mmm…"

"Yeah, yeah." She pretended to be watching the TV, but as always, her mind wandered to Ty. She'd been without sex for a while—months now—and ignoring the firm contours of this happily moaning man's warm back was an impossibility. Especially when she'd already seen what they could do.

"That feels so bloody good," he groaned.

Kate heard in his voice that he was already poised to drop off to sleep. Beneath her palm, his muscles released the tension they'd arrived with. Kate siphoned away his restlessness and let herself get lost in idle thoughts.

This body was a ratings booster, no doubt about it, and Kate knew it intimately, almost every inch. Knowing it came with her job description as Woman Friday—someone to check skin for ticks, thorns, signs of illness, to disinfect cuts. Someone to pop dislocated joints back into place. Tend to fevers. To provide company in places so remote it drove a person mad just trying to comprehend it.

Her hand continued to circle its familiar, if borrowed, territory.

"Ty? Are you awake?"

He snored softly, as if in response.

"I don't know why we bother getting separate rooms," Kate said, knowing he wasn't listening. "It's a waste of money. We should just book a double. Or get adjoining rooms. Then at least you wouldn't have to wake me up every damn night. You could just waltz on in and commandeer my bed like you always do."

Kate had a fantasy about these motel incidents, about Ty slipping in while she was asleep and rousing her as he slid under the covers beside her. She imagined his long body pressing into the length of hers, his mouth finding hers in the dark, as familiar and easy as their rapport. Her palms would race down his shoulders and back, over his hips, his ass, taking in all the shapes of him. She imagined slipping her hands inside his underwear, just as he rolled on top of her, his intention and his need unmistakable. Kate lived for feeling needed, and the idea set her body on fire. She imagined his sounds, as well, the same as the ones he made when he took his boots off at the end of a long stretch of hiking or ate a restaurant meal after three days with barely anything in his stomach. That's how he'd sound when she wrapped her fingers around him, or her lips, or as he slid into her. Beautiful.

The motions of her hand on Ty's back and her wayward thoughts hypnotized Kate, and she almost screamed with shock when the bedside alarm clock began to buzz. She fumbled before managing to switch off the screeching device, then prodded Ty back to lucidity. Oddly enough, once he'd fallen asleep in her bed, even that industrial-strength siren couldn't reliably rouse him.

He groaned. "That was *not* forty minutes."

"No, that was forty-three minutes. Come on." She poked his butt with her finger. "Time to get up." She abandoned him to head to the shower.

TY TURNED OVER AFTER the bathroom door clicked shut. He stared up at the texture of the cheap ceiling plaster, illuminated in rainbow fits and starts by the droning television. Kate's water turned on and he heard her almighty yawn. There was a cold patch of skin on his back where her hand had been.

He thought back to the stupid conversation they'd had in the bar, about what they were to each other, everything but lovers. What he felt for Kate went far beyond familiarity and trust and partnership, beyond sexual attraction, too. It was wrapped up in how he felt around her. Calm, but *alive*. After growing up in the suffocating vacuum left in the wake of his sister's death, Ty had emerged into adulthood starved for human energy. He'd found it in dozens of half-assed relationships with animated but hollow women— women who appeared dynamic but were really just terrified of being alone. But Kate…her energy ran deep. She was driven. She practically vibrated with passion, but it was contained. Focused. Sometimes Ty wanted to wrap himself around her and feel contained, too, for a change.

Of course he wanted other things, as well. So many nights spent lying beside her during these early-morning bed hijackings, wishing he could turn over. Roll onto his back and feel her hands, curious and fearless and demanding, touching him. He twitched from the thought of it. Kate might technically be his employee, but she was also the ringmaster in their two-man circus. She was the one in control, dishing out directives, and he wanted that little shot-caller in bed. He craved the hands of that capable, judgmental taskmaster on his body—assessing him and demanding his obedience.

Sighing at his own ridiculous lack of professionalism, Ty sat up and clicked the TV off. He went to the bathroom door and knocked.

Kate's shout came through the hiss of the water and the shoddy pressed wood of the door. "What?"

"What color is the shower curtain, Katie?"

A theatrical groan. "It's opaque, Ty."

He pushed the door in, and was smacked in the face by the steam rolling out from behind the partition. It was a wonder Kate didn't boil herself alive, she took such insanely hot showers. But she'd done her time in glacial rivers, and gone days without so much as a wet hand towel to wipe her face. She'd earned these indulgences.

"Are you excited?" she asked over the din, and Ty heard a shampoo bottle snap open or closed.

He closed the toilet lid and sat. "Yeah. You?"

"Of course. I've never been dogsledding before."

"They sounded skeptical."

"Yeah, well, they should be," she said. "They wanted us to train for a week, so the dogs would get to know us. We're giving them four hours."

"We've done madder things."

"You don't have to tell me. I am a little nervous, though." Her steam-flushed face appeared at the edge of the curtain, hair dripping water over her cheek and onto the bath mat. "Those dogs are brutal. I watched some videos online—it's like kicking apart drunks in a bar fight, keeping them in line. Drunks with fangs."

"I'm up for it." Few things intimidated Ty.… Decisions petrified him, but with Kate around, happily calling the shots for the show, he was mercifully stripped of that duty. He was in charge of taking the actual risks, the ideal job description for a man who lived to tempt fate. Anything for a thrill. Anything to keep him safely distracted from the static buzzing in his restless skull.

Kate's head disappeared behind the curtain. "Bet you're ready for today to be over with, old-timer. Ready for some time off?"

Ty laughed. "Only in this business does thirty-one count as old age." Still, thirty-one…when had that happened? Ty's life and career had progressed through a series of flukes— the reckless acceptance of others' dares, the pursuit of goals selected by the flip of a coin or the toss of a dart. On-screen, Ty was the picture of focused self-assurance, but demand something as simple as a choice of restaurants from him and he froze. He'd gotten good at hiding it, always defer- ring to his date's choice of destination, ordering whatever special the waitstaff suggested. Ty was a pro at passing off paralyzing indecision as easygoing chivalry.

Kate's voice cut through his thoughts. "Okay, get out."

Ty closed the door behind him, the dry air of the main room feeling arctic after the sauna of Kate's shower. The water shut off and he listened as she pushed the clacking curtain rings to one side. He was good. He didn't try and picture the scene. Not this time, anyhow.

She emerged five minutes later smelling like her usual postshower self. Lotion, he guessed. Nothing flowery, just clean. Like laundry. Ty wanted to toss her across the bed's rumpled sheets and get himself slapped.

"What are you sighing about?" She toweled her wet hair and looked at him with those stormy blue eyes.

"Nothing."

"All right then, get your dog-kicking boots on, Grizzly Adams. Let's go make a masterpiece."

3

"THERE! THAT'S IT!"

Ty looked to where Kate was pointing, spotting the sign for Grenier's Sled Supply and Excursions up ahead on the winding, pine-lined road. He turned them into the drive, their rented truck bucking in the deep, slush-filled potholes. Unseen dogs barked hysterically.

Kate the Guerilla PA was out the door before Ty even brought them to a complete stop. She strode toward the gruff lumberjack of a man who'd emerged from the converted farmhouse. The two met halfway in a long handshake, and Ty watched Kate launch into her spiel, whipping out waiver forms and other legal inevitabilities from her laptop bag. There were papers to be signed regarding their safety, the equipment's safety, the price of the rentals versus the negotiated cost of flashing the business's sign and giving them a name drop in the show. Thank goodness for Kate. That sort of stuff bored Ty to tears.

He gathered the two packs and the camera gear from the back of the truck and joined the conversation, glancing between them. "All right?"

Kate did the introductions. "Ty, this is Jim Grenier. Jim, this is Dom Tyler."

"Of course. Me and my wife love your show, Mr. Tyler." Jim Grenier seemed to be telling the truth, or a decent facsimile of it.

"Cheers. And 'Ty' is fine, by the way." He accepted the older man's hand and shook it with a manly curtness. This was what men wanted from Ty—what his on-screen persona promised. No nonsense, a man's man. Ty always delivered it, too, knowing men were by far his harshest critics…particularly specimens like this one, real frontiersmen, rare in this day and age. Ty scanned Grenier, his rugged clothes and boots, weather-beaten face and full beard. Ty's duty was to acquiesce, to demonstrate his enthusiasm and gratitude for the knowledge on offer, but never to come off as a softie. Plenty of these guys were dying for a chance to knock a hotshot television survival host down a few pegs. Ty thought this fellow seemed okay, though. Skeptical, but amused. It beat open contempt, at any rate. Plus Ty felt he should get a pass on this one—what did an Aussie know about dogsledding?

"Let's go meet the team," Jim said, and he led them back to a paddock filled with barking dogs. All huskies, some white Siberian, some gray and more wolfish-looking, some tethered and others roaming free. All of them sized Ty and Kate up with ethereal blue or pale brown eyes.

The next few hours were spent getting a crash course in the sport. They'd both done their homework but it was a tough skill to pick up and run with—the dogs snarled and snapped, prone to infighting and distraction. After a few hours, though, Ty and Kate were confident. Kate excelled at shouting and rushing the dogs when they began to jump on one another. She played a very convincing alpha female, even though a few of these dogs weighed a good seventy-plus pounds, most of it muscle. Kate was slender, healthy and fit but not jacked, yet when her mind was set on something she turned as ferocious and unrelenting as a junkyard dog herself.

"You're a little *too* good at that," Ty said as she reasserted order following a scuffle.

"You forget I had six older brothers."

Ty smirked at her. "And just how many of your brothers are dead again, Kate?"

Her lips pursed into an irritated frown. "None," she admitted.

"And yet you still talk about your family in the past tense."

"Yeah, well being out here with you makes Dorchester, Massachusetts, feel like a lifetime ago, Ty."

He wanted to pry, but held his tongue. Kate only ever spoke about her past in vague or elusive terms. She didn't act as if she was hiding anything, just turned weary and contemptuous when the topic came up, as though she were being asked to recite the multiplication table or some other mundane bit of information. But because he knew she was stuck with him, both physically and professionally, Ty didn't mind salting the wound. If she didn't deck him first, one day she'd slip and finally give him some insight into why she was the way she was. He might even return the favor.

By midmorning they had the gear loaded onto the sled and Ty mounted one camera at the front for some good action shots. Overcast sky and freezing temperatures aside, the grueling work had found them ditching their jackets before long and Ty was down to his undershirt. They were invited inside, and Ty sat in the Greniers' kitchen and watched Kate eat a woodsman's breakfast with Jim. She shoveled waffles into her mouth with one hand and waved a Dictaphone back and forth, asking syrup-muffled questions and recording Jim's answers between bites of sausage. It was all potential voice-over filler for the episode. As usual, Ty wasn't eating.

The rumbling in his stomach alone told him this was day three. The goose from day one was a distant memory and he didn't bother counting the eggs. He eyed Kate's coffee with longing.

"I think that'll do it," she said with a gracious smile at their host, clicking the recorder off. "We'll see you tonight around eight. Ty, I'm just going to go check the truck." She nodded to them both before heading outside.

Ty stood and gave the older man's hand a final shake. "Thanks for all your help, Jim. I hope we'll do you proud out there."

"Well, best of luck. Your wife seems extremely capable. I'm sure you'll be fine."

Ty laughed. "We're not a couple," he said, enjoying the look of surprise on Jim's face. "You've seen my show. You really think I can keep up with *that?*" He thrust a thumb in the direction of Kate's departure.

"Well, she's certainly…energetic."

"You don't know the half of it," Ty said, careful to keep his tone free of innuendo. He tendered his thanks one last time and stepped back into the cold, damp air. *Wife,* he thought with a grin. People made that mistake a lot, despite the fact that neither of them wore a ring. But it was no wonder that they must seem that way. In Ty's opinion, making this show was just a years-long honeymoon, one lacking substantially in the consummation department. Other than that frustrating exception, if this was a marriage, he couldn't find a reason to complain. If anything, his bachelor eyes strayed only when he mustered a concerted effort.

He made his way around the house to where one of Jim Grenier's staff was hitching the eight-dog team to their waiting sled. He pointed Ty and Kate off in the direction of the trail they'd be following. It formed a fifty-mile loop through the woods, and the team had made the journey hundreds of times. Even if Ty got them lost, the dogs would bring them home as though on autopilot.

Kate pulled a furry Inuit cap over her head and fixed Ty with an adventure-hungry eye that sparkled even under cloud cover. "Ready?"

"Always."

She climbed aboard behind him and bracketed her arms around his sides, grabbing hold of the bar at the front of the sled. "God, I hope I don't puke on you, Ty. I can't believe how many waffles I ate."

Ty smiled and shook his head. "You unholy bitch." He gave the shout to the dogs and they were off.

THE FIRST HALF HOUR of the trip flashed by in a snowy blur, fun and exhilarating. The following hour was bearable, though Kate was growing cold, fast. She flexed her fingers inside her gloves, willing her blood to move.

Ty turned his head to catch her eye. "You hanging in there?"

"Bit chilly."

"Never let yourself sweat in a cold climate," he lectured in an annoying, matronly tone. It was a lesson he'd imparted on the show at least a dozen times now. Of course it was exactly what Kate had done during the sled prep, leaving herself clammy and shivering now. Her wool sweater wasn't cutting it. Ty had managed to fumble into his jacket a little earlier, but hers was stashed way up front, pinned somewhere between their frame packs.

She squeezed herself close so Ty's body would block the wind. Plus she always liked his smell on day three. Must have been a positive pheromone match, since musky, unshaven, disheveled men were not Kate's usual taste. Ty wasn't to her typical taste in many respects, but damn if he didn't feel plain old good right now—big and sturdy and strong. Crazy-strong. Kate remembered with a shudder all the nerve-racking climbing videos she'd tracked down when she was first courting Ty for the job. No ropes, no axe, no harness—just climbing shoes, insanely strong fingers and arms, and a complete lack of common sense. She squeezed him tighter, thinking about it.

"All right back there?" he asked.

"Yup. Just trying to hang on."

He bellowed a mushing order to the dogs and the sled charged ever faster through the woods.

Ty's daredevil tendencies hadn't changed a jot since he'd landed the show, and neither had his reputation. People with too much time on their hands argued incessantly on message boards about whether he was the real deal or not, but Kate knew the truth. Ty would do anything as long as it was technically survivable. It went beyond adrenaline to something Kate couldn't understand, some cosmic game of chicken he lived and breathed. Ty drove safely, but he never wore a seat belt. He walked alarmingly close to construction sites, as though daring a stray wrench to fall and clock him on the head. He frequented the shadiest bars in L.A. and rushed in to break up other men's fights. Kate bet he picked the most dented cans at the supermarket, just to see if he'd come down with botulism. The world's oddest, dullest game of Russian roulette.

The only time Ty ever showed hesitation was when there were kids around. Take him to the beach for a so-called relaxing afternoon and he turned into a sheep dog, alert and aware of everything going on around him, as if the theme from *Jaws* was playing on his own private frequency. Kate, on the other hand, was made to adhere to every precaution available during filming and travel.

Ty craned his head around as Kate rested hers between his shoulders. "Are you falling asleep on me?"

"No, just hiding in your slipstream."

"We can pull over if you need a break. You need to pee? You drank enough blooming coffee back there."

"Nah. The ice fishing site can't be more than another hour. I can hold it. Beats stopping these guys and risking another fight. I can't wait till we can ditch them at the lake. Although all this footage will be badass."

"Delicious, hot, fresh-brewed coffee," Ty murmured, ignoring her shoptalk.

"I know, Hercules. Just a few more hours. What's on your menu?" Kate asked, referring to his dinner once filming wrapped and he could break his fast.

"Depends on if I get my fish, I suppose. But I suspect there will be potatoes involved. And dessert," he added. "And beer."

"I'm just going to have a salad," Kate replied, cruel as always. "I've been eating far too much on this trip."

"Ooh, she thinks she's so clever."

Kate glanced at the strip of gray between the trees lining the trail. "The sky's getting dark, isn't it?"

"I suppose.… 'S'all right, though," Ty said. "It's always good to add a little extra misery to the show."

"The viewers do love watching you suffer," she agreed. They frequently got letters and emails complaining when certain episodes didn't strike the audience as miserable enough to be believable. They seemed to like watching strikingly good-looking people like Ty struggle.

"Not just the viewers, Kate. I see you behind that tripod, smiling under your stupid golf umbrella with your flasks of hot-bloody-chocolate."

"It's tea today," she corrected in a languid voice. "You want a sip?" She grabbed the thermos from a compartment near her feet and waved it in his periphery.

He laughed. "God, piss off."

Kate wrapped her arms around his waist so she could unscrew the cap without falling off the sled, and managed to take a long drink. "Oh man, that's good. Who knew you could find decent chai in Saskatch—"

A shocking crack split the air in tandem with an almighty lurch. Kate lost track of reality as gravity flipped and she was suddenly suspended in the air. She heard a harsh grunt, the sound of Ty's wind being knocked out, and she felt herself gasp as she collided with the trunk of a tree. Then, blackness.

BLOODY HELL.

Lying immobile in the snow, Ty watched the overturned sled being dragged away at full tilt by the dog team until they disappeared around the next bend. Half the supplies he and Kate had put on board had come loose and were strewn across the trail for several yards. It took him nearly an entire minute to catch his breath and get control of his limbs, but he was relieved to find that nothing felt broken. He fumbled to his feet in the four-inch-deep slush and looked around.

"Katie?" He hiked back a little ways along the trail, shouting her name. Apprehension mounted when she didn't shout back. There was a fallen limb in the middle of the path, and Ty felt sure that it had been buried in the snow before the sled had struck it and driven it up into the air, throwing them off. Thank God it hadn't impaled either of them. Still, where was Kate?

He didn't spot her until he doubled back. His blood ran cold when he caught sight of her gray sweater and jeans at the woods' edge. She lay crumpled beneath a tree, motionless. Ty was used to chemical rushes—he was practically addicted to them—but the panic surging through his body stopped him dead in his tracks. Fear wrung the air from his lungs but Ty commanded his muscles to work, broke through the paralysis and into a sprint.

"Kate!" He slid to a sloppy halt beside her still body. Ty could taste copper in his own mouth when he spotted the trickle of scarlet running across her pale skin from her mouth to disappear into her hair. He was transported in a single breath, ripped back in time twenty-five years and nine thousand miles to a warm summer day, a beach outside Sydney. He saw his little sister's hollow expression, her vacant eyes as blue as the ocean. He felt his own life fracture and scatter all over again as he stared at Kate's white face.

"Kate. Katie." He yanked his gloves off and tossed them aside. Taking hold of her jaw, he searched for signs of life. He just about died of relief when he felt a pulse beating in her neck, strong and steady.

"Katie." He smoothed her hair off her face and wiped the blood from her skin as best he could. He lost himself for a moment to overwhelming emotions—relief and fear and gut-wrenching guilt, a lifetime of stale grief made fresh. He lowered his face to her shoulder and concentrated on her breathing. Each exhalation calmed him, rooted him back in the present. Kate was alive, but she wasn't necessarily safe. Not out here, not if she was hurt.

Just as Ty began conceiving a plan for how best to get her to the safety team, her eyes opened.

"Oh thank Christ!" he boomed into the sky.

"Ty…" She sounded groggy, but she was okay. *She was okay.*

"Bloody hell, Katie, you scared me."

"Where are we?"

He looked around, needing a second to recall there was a world beyond the face of the woman he'd just nearly lost. "The dogsled trail."

"Right… And the dogs?"

"A long ways away now." He stroked her hair, still frantic. "How do you feel? Is anything broken?"

She frowned. "I'm not sure. Let me try and stand up."

"Careful." Ty thought he might pass out himself, she'd given him such a fright.

"Ow," she said, making it to kneeling.

"What?"

"Just bumps, I think. Nothing major… Oh God!" She stood up in a flash.

Ty whipped his head around, scanning for bears and avalanches. "What?"

"The equipment—the cameras! Do we have any cameras?" She looked overwrought. Unbelievable.

"Jesus, I don't know. The sled dumped about half our stuff. Worry about it in a minute—let's make sure you're okay."

"I am. I feel fine." She touched her lips and studied the blood on her fingers, made an irritated face and wiped it on her jeans.

Ty saw her arms shaking faintly beneath her sweater and he slipped his jacket off. "Here."

She took it, still distracted. "Thanks. What a mess." Her calculating eyes scanned the area, telling him she was already back in work mode.

"Are you sure you're okay? Do you feel any bumps? You could be concussed."

"I'm fine. Let's just get ourselves assembled." She trudged toward their jettisoned supplies.

Ty, however, didn't want to regroup just yet. Sense had been knocked into him by the incident. It had whiplashed his brain, sending the fear that had been niggling at the back of his mind for a very long time crashing to the forefront, demanding his attention. This ridiculous project—this stupid TV show—had nearly killed his best friend.

Beneath the subsiding shock, primitive synapses burst to life in his chest. Possessive ones. Their energy jumbled with the fear and guilt, making Ty's blood run fast and hot—faster and hotter than even he was comfortable with. He watched Kate's body working, already recovered from its trauma, and an instinct rose inside him, sharp and insistent. It burned through the angst and replaced it with other urges—urges not just to protect and shield this woman, but to possess her, to take her. To tear away that lone wall that kept them from being everything to one another.

A SHORT DISTANCE AWAY, Kate took a deep breath and made an inventory of the items she could see. She pulled Ty's proffered jacket on, glad for the warmth and for a reassuring layer of protection. She needed to turn her attention back to the show, because in truth, the accident had scared her witless. She'd grown plenty used to adrenaline rushes since she'd taken this job, but this was a thrill too far—the closest she'd ever flirted with a major injury in all the time they'd been doing this. Too close for comfort. Even Ty seemed disturbed, and that in itself was scary.

More than a mere mortal, however, Kate was first and foremost a professional. No way she was going to stand around wasting time now that the damage had already been done. One of the cameras had been pitched in the accident. Kate unzipped its padded case and breathed a sigh of relief to find it in one piece. The show would go on.

"Good news, boss." She held it up to show Ty, but he didn't respond.

Ty's eyes seemed to be looking through her, his energy even more intense than usual. His boots sloshed as he walked to her. She watched him swallow deeply, expression fraught as though he were unraveling.

"Yeah, Ty?"

He swallowed again, his eyes darting back and forth between hers. Something fierce was brewing behind the deceptive blue-green calm.

"It's okay. We're both okay," she began, but his face told her the words weren't registering. His arms rose and encircled her, cautiously at first, then he pulled her tight against his chest. One broad hand cupped the back of her head, pressing her face into his neck, the other fisting the oversize coat.

"Dear God," he said, his mouth pushed so hard into her hairline that it sounded as if his voice were coming from inside her skull. "I never imagined I'd come so close to losing you."

"I'm fine, Ty." She tried to pull away but his embrace was tight and needy, so she let him hold on. She'd never seen him like this, so rattled. It embarrassed her a little, intimidated her a lot.… His breaths came fast and shallow, and Kate returned the hug with her free arm, hoping to calm him. "It's okay." She rubbed his back, an upright version of what she did when his insomnia drove him into her bed.

Ty's body loosened. His hands released their death grip and he let her go, stepping back a pace and staring at her. His eyes were round and unfocused. Kate caught the corner of his mouth twitching.

She zipped the camera back in its bag and set it aside, looked nervously up at Ty. "Are you okay?"

Shaking slightly, his hands cupped her shoulders, the way they had dozens of times before. She felt her eyes widen and she squirmed as his palms slid up to her neck.

"This so isn't the time, Ty."

He ignored her protest, thumbs pressing against her pulse

points as the script dictated. Lips on her temple. Snow began to fall.

"Knock it off," she said.

"What?"

"Your stupid flirting shtick."

His mouth slid farther still, until she heard his soft voice right in her good ear. "I'm not playing right now."

She faltered. "Don't be a jerk."

He shifted so their noses touched, right on cue. "Then tell me what you want me to be," he whispered, his lips grazing hers. That wasn't part of the script.

"What I want you to be?" she whispered back, flubbing her lines.

"Who am I to you?"

The Shift again, but this time it was different. Intense, and not a game. All she managed to say was, "Who are you?"

"Yeah." She felt Ty's smile more than she could see it from this close, heard it in his words. "What am I, Katie? Your boss? Your friend?"

"Both," she mumbled. Her heart had lodged in her throat like a rubber ball, cutting off her oxygen.

"Could I ever be more?"

"Are you about to kiss me?" she asked, dumbstruck, heart pounding. She'd never been any good at playing coy.

"Are you about to let me?"

She trembled. "I dunno. Frigging find out."

Ty's thumbs slid up past her jaw and pressed hard into her cheeks, just as his lips parted and took her lower one between them.

A kiss. An actual, technical kiss.

Kate's eyes closed and a deep shiver passed through her body when she heard and felt a soft moan escape from Ty's throat. A hunk of snow fell from her collar down the back of her sweater, the wet chill balancing the heat of Ty's mouth. He kissed her again. She kissed back. He angled his jaw and opened his mouth wider, his tongue timidly flirting with hers, then going deeper, bolder. Kate's hands were dangling limply at her sides and she got control of them, pushed them through the ends of Ty's jacket's long sleeves. Once they were free, she ran them up his hard, bare arms and settled them in his hair, knocking his hat off. His mouth felt dangerous—demanding and hot and wet, and he tasted just as she'd always known he would. Kate forgot the accident and her professionalism in a flash of hormonal amnesia. She wanted more. She wanted to taste every inch of him, and to be sampled by his mouth in return, all over her body. How many nights had she lain mere inches from this mouth, listening as Ty whispered sleepy words in the dark of a tent or the back of a van? How many nights had she spent wondering if they'd ever take things too far? She'd imagined this moment a hundred times—a thousand times. And she'd been wrong. It was so much better than her imagination had ever dared to hope.

The kiss deepened and intensified. Wet snowflakes landed on Kate's flushed face and she held in a groan as one of Ty's strong hands cupped her head. His body pressed into hers until they stumbled back a step, her shoulders pushed hard against a tree trunk. An invisible floodgate opened between them. Ty's kissing turned shallow as the noises he seemed helpless to control escaped him. Moans and dark, heavy breaths, grunts and sighs. His hand tightened in her hair and suddenly he wrenched his lips from hers, moving them to her temple, close to her good ear. His breath steamed against her skin.

"God, Katie."

An old sensation crept in to banish the passion, cooling her. Fear. She pushed him back a pace. "Don't."

He stared down at her face. "Don't what?"

Don't make me fall for you. "Just don't do that again." She licked her lips, still burning and tender where his had savaged them. An icy trickle of water ran down her back as she pulled away from the tree, a cold, cruel finger tracing her spine.

Ty's voice turned soft and melancholy. "Sure. Sorry." He turned away and strode to the scattered cargo.

For a half a minute she just watched him, suppressing a hundred urges—to call out to him, tell him she changed her mind, tell him to go to hell, tell him to come back here and take more, whatever he wanted. Instead she followed suit, wandering around and gathering their stuff. Each rescued item rooted her more firmly in rational thought, wrapped her in safety, kept the fear at bay. Kept the old Kate at bay, the one who'd let her heart rule her head in her teens and early twenties, led her down too many painful paths in pursuit of affection from men who had none to offer. Grasping, needy, white trash Kate Sullivan, little miss daddy-abandonment issues from the wrong side of a town she'd never make it out of… Only she had. She'd edited out all the bad bits of herself, ditched her Boston accent and her last name and her suffocating clinginess, reinvented herself. She was different now, and Ty was like a test. If she followed her body's wishes she'd be gambling with too much—her job, her closest friendship, her new identity. And over what? If she knew Ty at all, it'd be a couple days' or a couple weeks' excitement, then he'd go cold. She'd seen him do it with enough women—women far more fascinating than Kate—and she refused to be the next in line.

She watched his back as he pulled on some extra layers he'd scavenged from the remaining cargo. A tremor shuddered from deep inside her chest, and in its wake she felt the sweet relief of knowing she'd held fast to the one thing that kept her in control. Kate found her coat and took Ty's off, zipping herself into the familiar. She clad her body in warm down, waterproof nylon, her heart in the iron and steel forged by old pain and thickened by every person she'd ever lain down and played the sucker for.

You've already got my life, Dom Tyler. She stared at him across the churned-up snow. *Don't think for a second you'll take my heart.*

4

"SNOW'S PICKING UP," Ty said, looking in front of them, then behind. "What do you reckon? Turn back and head for the Greniers'?"

Kate shook her head, glad for a rational topic to refocus her attention. "The safety crew's closer by now…it's got to be." She pulled her hat on and glanced around, noting how thick and dense the snow had indeed become. "But there's a fork in the trail…it splits into two loops and they don't reconnect for quite a ways. I don't know which route is right, and the map's in your pack."

"Which is halfway home by now," Ty sighed, looking in the direction the dogs had long since disappeared in.

Kate nodded. "Along with the GPS and satellite phone. As far as the safety crew can tell, we're making steady progress. They won't even suspect anything's wrong until this afternoon, when the dogs get back home ahead of schedule with no humans in tow."

"Bugger."

"Yeah, bugger. We need to move fast and find the fork before the snow covers the dogs' tracks." Kate sputtered out a frustrated breath. She forced herself into work mode, escaping thoughts of hypothermia, of Ty's mouth, of the ache he'd left in her body. They loaded all the supplies back into her pack and Ty shouldered it. Kate set the lone remaining camera up with its sun hood to keep the flakes from streaking the lens. Flicking the power on, she trained the viewfinder on Ty's head and shoulders as she trudged alongside him.

His posture shifted and he reclaimed some of the hostly professionalism he'd lost since the crash. He turned to address their future audience.

"Well, this is unexpected." He cleared his throat. "If the camera I mounted on the sled survived its trip back to town, you'll have noticed I didn't exactly go with it. That's not an uncommon way to find yourself suddenly lost in the Canadian bush, either. Every year, dozens of people get separated from their dogsleds just like this, and believe it or not, we didn't stage that."

Ty glanced at the dark woods surrounding them, the even grayness of the sky above. Great flakes of sticky snow clung to his eyebrows and sideburns and flew into his face, making him squint. "We're out of simulation mode now, I'm afraid, and right up against it in a proper survival situation. How's that for a season finale? I wish I could tell you I knew how far I am from our safety crew's camp, but I can't. I think it's about one o'clock now, and if I don't come across them in the next couple hours, I'm going to have to change strategies and start working on a shelter. It looks like there could be a nasty late-season storm coming through. It's not just me trapped out here, either," he added, pointing to the camera. "The crew's here, too, obviously, and I'm not taking any risks with their safety."

Ty paused so the commentary could be cut cleanly during editing before he continued. "What you at home didn't see," he said to the lens, "was that my camerawoman and production assistant, Kate Somersby, finally let me kiss her after two years of torturous cock-blocking."

"Two and a half," Kate corrected after a pause, against her better judgment.

"Two and a half, my fact-checker is telling me. I can say for the record now that she tastes like honey and some sort of exotic spice."

"That's just my tea." She tried to mask how shy he was making her feel, keeping the camera pressed to her eye, a shield against the intimacy he was trying to draw her into.

Ty continued his narration. "And when she ran her fingers through my hair, I wanted to pin her against that tree and make her beg me to take her."

"Stop it." Kate halted and lowered the camera. Strange energy twitched in the nest of nerves in her lower belly. "Don't joke about that."

"I'm not."

She resumed walking so she wouldn't have to face him.

"I wouldn't joke about that. I've wanted that for too bloody long to find it funny."

"Sounded like a joke to me," she snapped.

"I'm sorry, then. But it's not."

"Fine. Just keep it to yourself. I don't feel that way about you."

"No?" For once there was no tease in Ty's voice, just resounding, questioning disappointment.

"No. Believe it or not, at least one straight woman on this planet isn't looking to melt into a puddle just because the great Dom Tyler deigned to kiss her."

Ty's eyebrows knitted. "Well, don't make me sound like a colossal wanker about it."

"Check your track record, Ty. Milk keeps longer than your relationships, and I'm not exactly gunning to be the next thing that goes sour for you. Maybe you've forgotten, but I'm your partner and your friend. And your employee."

"You're also the woman who lets me crawl into her bed in the middle of the night."

She pursed her lips. "This show has to go on, Ty. Which means you have to sleep on occasion. Which means I do what I need to to make that happen."

"You care about this show a lot, don't you?" Ty asked.

Kate nodded, not meeting his eyes.

"What's the most important part of it, to you?"

How thoroughly it lets me avoid cultivating actual relationships and putting down roots. "I just like being a part of something, Ty. I like being useful and needed and depended on."

Ty was quiet for a while and when he spoke, he sounded older. Tired. "I need to change a few things about your job description, Kate."

Her blood chilled. She wiped the melting snowflakes from her eyelashes and looked at him, wary. "What do you mean?"

"I think you should stay home from now on. From the excursions."

Kate felt her heart race into overdrive, this pronouncement infinitely more terrifying than any survival scenario she'd ever come along for. Her brain supplied words Ty hadn't actually spoken, filled them in from a script she'd been living out her entire life. *I don't need you. I'm leaving you behind.* All at once, she was ready to flee and cry and scream and attack.

She shook her head, awestruck, grasping for control of her temper. "You can't do that, Ty."

"I have to after what just happened."

"Are you *firing* me?"

"I didn't say that. I'm just saying you're off filming. You

can keep the rest of your job, just not this." Ty waved his arm to encompass the dreary landscape.

Kate felt a tightness in her chest, a sensation of suffocating dread. "No. No. You can't just…ditch me." She heard the old Kate in those words and cringed at how needy she sounded.

"It's not ditching. It's just… This can't ever happen again, Kate. I'm sorry. Everything else you do for me, you can still do that. But once we get back and start producing the next season, I'm not letting you be a part of the shoots."

"What, you'll just do it all by yourself?"

"Maybe…or I'll hire somebody. Somebody…" Ty trailed off, eyes focused over Kate's shoulder as though the words he sought were hovering behind her.

"What? Somebody better trained?" she demanded. "Somebody competent, or—"

"No, just not you, okay?"

"You can't do this, Ty." The pleading quality had hijacked her voice again and Kate felt another pang of disgust. She hated herself for turning so suddenly pathetic, hated Ty for having the power to make her this way. "You just can't do this."

Ty smiled, tight and sad. "It's my show. I think you'll find I can."

That proclamation drove a spike into Kate's heart, and before she could stop them, words were tumbling out of her, shrill with anger. "I can't believe you're being this selfish."

"Not wanting you to get hurt is selfish, suddenly?"

"This is my life! This show is my *life*."

He huffed out a frustrated sigh and shook his head in a patronizing way that brought Kate's blood to a rolling boil. She stopped and set the camera on its case in the snow, rubbed her face.

He halted a few paces ahead and turned. Kate couldn't make out his expression through the heavy flakes. "We have to keep moving, Katie. And we need to stay close. The visibility's going to hell."

She barely heard the words. She was six months ahead of the present, picturing herself waving goodbye to Ty as he left for the next season's locations, left her behind, left whatever it was they were together behind without looking back. *See you, Kate. I'll send you a postcard.*

"Kate?"

She shook her head, tried to clear it, but succeeded only in scrambling the pain and hurt, redoubling it. All the emotions she usually blocked out were finding weak spots, poking through the holes in her armor.

"I'm not changing my mind on this, Kate. I'm sorry."

That last word shoved her right over the edge and Kate found herself doing the only thing that felt right—she strode forward and pushed him. A harmless shove, then another that sent him back a step. Then a flurry of angry, ineffective fists to his chest. Ty let it go on for a few seconds and then grabbed her wrists and steadied her.

"Kate, stop."

"Take back what you said—about gutting my job and wrecking my life!"

"This isn't your life. That was your life, back there." He nodded in the direction they'd come from, where the sled had flipped. "That thing you almost lost—for a television program. That's your life, and I just about got you killed just now. It's over. Nothing's worth that."

She jerked her elbows, trying to break his grip but standing no chance. "You can't just decide that!"

"Yeah, I can."

"Goddamn it, Ty, where is this coming from? From one sled accident in three seasons of shooting? From…from the fact that I told you not to kiss me?" The last couple words came out a mumble.

His eyes dropped back to hers. "No. I just can't let you endanger yourself for this. For me." His hold slackened and Kate yanked her hands back.

Panicking, she tried a different approach. "You're over-reacting because you're freaked out. But I'm fine!" She patted herself down, her shoulders, ribs, thighs. "I'm fine! And this isn't just your show. This is mine, too, and you know it. All of it, especially out here."

He cast his gaze to the snow between their feet. "I'm sorry, but I'm not changing my mind on this."

"I can't believe this." She crossed her arms over her chest.

"It's just a stupid show, Katie."

How could he say that? This stupid show, as he called it, was the sun Kate's life had orbited around these past two and a half years. She paused only a moment, just long enough to pull her glove off before she hit him again. Hard this time, an open palm across his face that jerked his head to the side with a snap and left a mean red mark blossoming beneath the heavy stubble on his jaw.

"Kate—"

"I've signed a hundred waivers to risk my neck for this 'stupid show,'" she hissed. "You don't get to fire me because I almost get hurt making a program whose whole goddamn premise is trying to *frigging stay alive!* Of course it's dangerous! That's the point!"

"Calm down." Ty made a move to grab her flailing arms again but she pulled back, livid.

"No! I won't! You don't get to do this! I've put my blood and sweat into this. Literally. Five seasons, you said. You promised me five seasons or until they stop renewing us.

Five seasons of *this,* not me behind a desk in L.A. and you out here where all the good stuff happens."

"Then I lied, Katie. I changed my mind, okay?"

"Don't call me that!" She hadn't corrected his calling her Katie in a very long time. No one ever called her that, not even when she was a little kid. Lovable, perky girls were called Katie, not prickly ones. The nickname was wrapped inexorably up in Ty, in how she felt around him, and she couldn't hear it now. "How can you do this?"

"It's a show. It's a job. You'll find another job, if what I'm offering isn't enough." He exhaled heavily. "We'll tweak the terms and I'll get you an amazing severance package, okay? I mean, where are your priorities? Why can't you see how big a deal it is that you nearly lost your life back there?"

Can't you see that you're *my life now?*

The silence that rang out in the wake of the shouting was deafening. Stomping back to the camera, Kate dusted off the snow and zipped it into its case, then set off along the trail. She could just see Ty's red jacket in her periphery. Just as well he was on her bad ear's side. She didn't much feel like hearing anything he might have to say.

The flakes fell around them, silent and steady. Kate forced herself back into professional mode and filled her overheated head with concerns of actual survival, not just the canned and dramatized variety. Ty was right about the visibility. Kate's pack contained a flare gun, but there was no point setting one off to try to alert the safety team, not in these conditions. At this rate the dogs' tracks would be obliterated within the hour. They needed to at least get to that fork, and fast.

The silence out here was eerie, broken only by the creaking of their boots in the wet snow. Trudging a few paces behind her, Ty spoke, his muffled words wasted. He jogged a few steps to walk on her good side. "Kate?"

"Don't talk to me."

For a long time, the better half of an hour, he didn't. When he did speak again, all he said was, "We need to think about shelter."

Kate didn't reply at first. She got the camera out and handed Ty the empty case to carry. Flicking on the power, she trained the viewfinder on his tired face.

"Not now, Kate."

"Do your job," she said coldly. "I've always done mine."

Ty sighed and the look in his eyes was one of sad obedience. As he walked, Ty addressed the camera, informing the audience about Saskatchewan, about the unseasonable weather currently dogging them, about gear. Kate tuned out, lost in her own worries. Eventually Ty fell silent and she shut the camera off. They continued in heavy silence and even heavier snow.

Eventually Kate broke the long lapse in conversation. "This really doesn't look good." She stared at the ominous pewter sky swirling above them.

Ty shook his head in agreement. "We're not going to make it to the safety crew."

"No, we haven't even reached the fork." She thought for a moment. "Tent's on the sled."

"Yeah. We may need to build something."

Kate sighed, accepting her fate. At least this was their area of expertise, plus working kept her calm. She turned the camera back on. "Rolling."

"Jesus, Kate. Now?"

"Yeah, we've still got to bring home forty-two minutes' worth of airable footage. We're not giving up just because we lost the fishing spot. This is better, even—you're always complaining about authenticity."

The corner of his mouth twitched. "Fine. But don't think I don't suspect you're doing this to get out of helping." His attempt at reestablishing their old levity didn't stand a chance against Kate's current mood.

"What are you going to do, Ty? Fire me?" She hid the true bitterness of her words behind the lens, making them sound light and pithy, though she was still fuming. He may as well have fired her. That's exactly what it felt like. Still… Her track record for talking Ty into things was impressive, and if she could just be patient and let the shock of the accident fade, she might be able to change his mind about his ridiculous decision.

"Okay," Ty said to the camera. "I've decided that reaching the safety crew's not going to happen fast enough in this storm, so I've got to reprioritize and get a shelter assembled, in case I can't get out of here before tomorrow. The things I'm most concerned with are the cold and dampness. I need to get something built up off the ground—" he mimed a shape with his hands "—with a buffer against the wind, even if I don't have time to get four walls in place. We're working with a few more hours of so-called daylight, I'd guess. I'm also worried about a fire, since the film crew and I got pretty wet when the sled pitched us.

"Now, looking around—" he waved his arms around at the snowy, slushy scene, and Kate scanned it with the camera "—you wouldn't reckon we'd have much luck trying to get a fire going. But if you've watched this show enough times I hope I've taught you that you can almost always get a fire started even if the tinder's looking grim. Anyhow, I'm going to search for some wood for the shelter."

Kate and the camera followed as he surveyed the area for materials. The chances of finding anything looked very grim, indeed.

Ty paused his search after a few fruitless minutes to address the audience. "Now the axe that any adventurer worth his salt would bring with him on this kind of trip is, I'm sad to say, making its way back to the dogs' base camp at this very moment. And I can tell you, getting a shelter put up without an axe is going to be about ten thousand times harder." Ty sighed heavily, contemplating this. "The other option," he said, still walking, "is to build a snow den. It might seem contradictory, building a shelter out of snow when you're trying to stay warm and dry. But actually it's an ancient building technique, and the insulation the snow can—"

He paused, seeing that Kate was pointing over his shoulder. He turned.

"Oh," he said, spotting the neon orange sign posted at the edge of the trail. Kate zoomed in on its words and instructive arrow. Emergency Shelter, 1 km.

She aimed the camera back at Ty.

"My crew has a better idea, apparently," he said, and offered a glimmer of his trademark smile.

He set a quick pace and Kate followed him the half mile to their salvation, a shed-style building erected just a short way off the trail. It looked to be in decent shape, with the exception of a broken windowpane and a carpet of moss creeping up one side.

"Emergency shelter," Ty said, turning back to his future audience. "This just goes to show you that, in this day and age at least, getting stranded doesn't always mean slapping a lean-to together. If you find yourself lost on a trail or in a popular hunting or trapping area, you might be able to find a man-made place just like this one. Let's see what we're working with, here. I can see a chimney, at any rate, so let's hope that means we've got a woodstove."

He tested the knob of the mildly moldy front door and pushed.

"Eureka," he began, then ducked and stumbled backward, covering his head as a dozen black birds rocketed out of the door and past their shoulders. "Right." He took the camera from Kate and scanned the space with it before they ventured inside.

It was as big as a couple of toolsheds, eight feet by fifteen, Kate estimated. Ty's prayer had been answered—a squat wood-burning stove sat at the far end next to a small pile of gnarled lumber left by whoever had been sequestered here last. Someone had taken the time to build a shelf above the stove, and on it sat a banged-up tin pot and a chipped mug, as well as a pair of rusty double-A batteries and an ancient, mildewy hunting magazine.

"Oh, glorious!" Ty jogged to the stove, bending over then straightening up again, holding an abandoned axe in front of the camera lens. "It's dull, but I can't tell you how excited I am to see this." Kate watched Ty record more of their discovery and his commentary for a few minutes.

"Damn, this is lucky," she said when she could speak again. A wobbly-looking card table stood by the door, kept company by an aluminum folding chair. There was even a small single bed against the wall near the woodstove. It looked exceedingly utilitarian, a metal army-style cot with a slatted headboard. Kate didn't trust the moldy mattress on it one bit, but they had a sleeping bag with them, which could make it workable. A heck of a lot more workable than a frigging snow den.

"Welcome home, darling." Ty set the camera down and scanned the shelter with his hands on his hips. "This is a bloody blessing, eh?"

"Better check for rats," Kate said. They poked around but found only the evidence of the squatting birds. She pulled a roll of electrical tape out of her pack and secured an empty pretzel bag over the missing window pane.

"Smells a bit," she said, flaring her nostrils at the musk of rotting wood.

"Yeah, sorry." Ty walked to the bed, sat down with a groan of rusty springs. "I wanted to get you the honeymoon suite, but it was booked."

"Get us a fire going," Kate ordered, not wanting to think about such things as honeymoon suites right now. This man had, after all, just demoted her. And what it felt like, more than anything else, was a breakup. When he'd told Kate he wanted her off filming, what she'd really heard was, "I'm dumping you." And she'd never imagined a breakup could hurt this badly. If she started thinking about it now the pain would be too great to bear. She'd never cried in front of Ty and she'd be damned if she was going to start now.

"Actually, you get the fire going," Ty said, and he fished in Kate's pack for a moment then tossed her her lighter. "I'll go look for some decent wood for when that stuff runs out." He nodded at the selection of old firewood they'd inherited.

"Fine. Bag us a three-course meal, while you're at it," she said.

"As you wish." He disappeared with the axe, leaving Kate alone with not nearly enough distractions. She unstrapped the sleeping bag from her pack, tossed it across the bed and took a seat. Spinning her lighter's thumbwheel around and around, she got lost in the sparks.

God. This couldn't happen. This was her entire life, this show. Not being here, being a part of the real process, would be worse than getting fired outright…saying goodbye to Ty as he left for weeks at a time, off to do the things they'd always done together, as a pair. Now she'd be left in his dust, or worse, in the dust of some hateful replacement. Kate looked down, dropped the lighter and fisted her hands, letting her nails bite into her palms, letting the pain push away her urge to cry. She'd moved to L.A. expecting something a lot different from this—something a lot safer and cleaner and more glamorous. But damn if it hadn't grown on her. Damn if Ty hadn't grown on her.

Damn if she wasn't half in love with the bastard.

5

Ty TRUDGED THROUGH the ever-deepening snow, looking forward to pulling his slush-filled boots off as soon as he'd gathered enough wood to get them through the night. The flakes seemed to be getting bigger by the minute. He tendered a mental prayer to his ambiguous and unreliable higher power that the storm wouldn't get so bad that they couldn't travel the next day. Hunger had long since left him weak and dispirited and he didn't think he could take much more of this godforsaken wilderness.… Of course he'd finally decided to lose his nerve on the one shoot where quitting wasn't an option.

Kate's temper had him more nervous than the weather, though—he'd half expected lightning to shoot out of her eyes at him during that fight. He couldn't blame her for being angry. This *was* her show. She'd never failed to rise to any challenge since he'd taken her on as his assistant. Sometimes he felt he'd known her forever. Yet he could remember the first time they met as if it had been last week.

Ty hadn't yet found an office or apartment when the network had unexpectedly optioned his pilot, so Kate met him at his hotel on a typical sunny L.A. afternoon. She turned up at precisely the appointed hour, clad in a blazer and a pink, collared shirt, shiny pointy-toed shoes and pressed slacks. She looked as if she'd just stepped off the set of a soap opera in which she played a ballsy, no-nonsense, sex-kitten lawyer.

Ty shook her hand and watched her slip a glossy lock of her hair, complete with salon-fresh highlights, behind her ear. This was so not going to work.

He'd posted the job the previous afternoon in the online trade papers, and all he'd said was, "PA needed on location for new reality / survival program. Crap pay, great travel opportunities." He'd been hoping for maybe a beach bum kid, some twenty-something wannabe pro surfer with a taste for adventure and an up-for-it attitude. A hard worker, but relaxed and adaptable, competent with a camera and mics. Someone like himself, whose only dream was to get paid to travel and have fun. The woman who arrived that morning wasn't any of those things, as best Ty could tell.

"Tell me about your experience, Miss…Somersby," he said, squinting at the take-out menu he'd scribbled her name on the previous evening when she'd phoned. He tried to sound professional, but he really had no idea what he was doing. He'd never expected the channel to pick up the pilot he'd taped on a climbing acquaintance's beer-fueled dare. But a rival network had recently begun production on a similar series, and they'd been eager to try to beat the competition out of the gate. That Ty demanded little in the way of budget, schedule or staff had clinched the deal.

"I can do anything, Mr. Tyler," Kate said, her smile all unnaturally white even teeth framed in lip gloss. She took a seat on the hotel room's desk chair and Ty sat on the edge of the bed. "I'm highly organized and have no personal obligations, so I'm at your complete disposal, twenty-four hours a day."

"Well, that's certainly…accommodating. How old are you?" he asked.

"Twenty-six."

"Did you recently graduate from college?"

"No," she said, and Ty noticed her bubbling energy diminish by a degree. "I didn't go to college."

"Well, that's not a problem. Just making small talk. Do you like the woods?"

"I grew up in Massachusetts," she said, which meant nothing to Ty, literally hours off a plane from Sydney. "I've been camping and hiking before," she offered.

"You like camping?"

"Sure, it's fine. Like I said, I'll do anything."

Ty took a deep breath, knowing he needed to scare this girl straight, get her to back off and spare them both the embarrassment of an outright rejection. "Are you strong? Could you, say, carry a fifteen-pound camera on your shoulder for an hour at a time?"

"I'm sure I could," she said brightly, unruffled. "I go to the gym every morning."

"How about asthma? Allergies? Food requirements? This job demands a lot of exotic travel. You okay with centipedes and snakes and things?"

"I can handle anything you need me to."

Ty tried another angle. "What about family? Friends? You'd have to be away for months at a time."

Her smile was tight. "I'm not particularly attached to anyone, Mr. Tyler."

"'Ty' is fine."

"So is 'Kate.'"

"Right, I'll be honest with you, I don't think this is going to work out."

Her brows pinched together. "Why not?"

"Well, this job is really demanding, physically, for one."

"I'm sure you're not implying that I can't do this because I'm a woman."

Damn, was he? He didn't think so, but perhaps subconsciously, Ty'd pictured his PA as a man, that was true. "No, of course not."

"I'm glad to hear that."

"Yes, well… I'm just saying, this job's going to be very taxing, and the filming's going to be on location for days at a time. Maybe weeks. There could be wild animals and rough weather, even simulated shipwrecks or arctic conditions…"

"That sounds just fine." Kate offered another million-dollar smile, as if he'd just broken it to her that her company car wouldn't be the color she'd hoped.

Ty laughed tightly, growing exasperated. "I'm afraid I just don't see this working out, Miss…Somersby."

"Kate. And I do," she added, assertive. Hungry. "Why don't you give me a shot? A free trial?"

"I don't know."

"No one else could possibly do a better job for you than me," she said with an almost contemptuous confidence. "I can offer you round-the-clock assistance."

"It's not your availability I'm concerned about. This could be quite a dangerous job."

Kate leaned in, an intriguing gleam underscoring her stare. "Sounds thrilling."

Ty swallowed. "I must admit, you're very keen."

"I am."

He sighed, not sure what to do. She wasn't letting him turn her down gracefully, and he had no legitimate reason to deny her. Not yet, at least. And to be honest, the other candidates he'd met or talked to on the phone had seemed far less…*passionate* than this one.

He blew out a breath and rolled his shoulders. "Listen… Okay. What are you doing this weekend?"

"You tell me," she said, a glimmer of triumph already sparkling in her dark blue eyes.

"Right, then. Meet me here on Friday at two, and I'll give you a trial run through Sunday, okay? Then we'll see if this is a good fit."

"Excellent. Should I bring anything in particular?"

Ty thought for a moment and decided on a bit of strategic cruelty. "No, Kate, just come as you are… Maybe change your shoes. Something a bit more practical."

"Right." She drew a folio from an expensive-looking briefcase and made a note. "Two o'clock on Friday, then. I'm very much looking forward to it."

"So am I," Ty lied.

Two days later Kate had arrived at his door at one fifty-nine, knocking briskly. He answered it with his shirt still unbuttoned—he wasn't half as punctual as she was. She gave his bare chest a quick and businesslike once-over and launched into the matter at hand.

"Good afternoon, Dominic."

"'Ty,' please," he corrected, doing up the last of his buttons. "So I take it you haven't been snapped up by some young starlet, then?"

"Of course not. I'm very excited to get to work. What may I do for you?" she asked, glowing from her perfectly styled hair down past her argyle cardigan, right to the tiny buckles of her shiny black flats. Ty frowned. Those were a step closer to comfort than the gougers she'd had on the other day, but he'd assumed she'd turn up in sneakers… no matter. That was the evidence he'd been waiting for. Those would make it that much easier to get rid of her. Ty had planned this trip to last three days if need be, but he was sure now that they'd be done by sundown. Hell, once he outlined the particulars she'd probably be sprinting to her car, racing back downtown in ten seconds flat.

"We're going camping, actually, Miss Somersby." He grinned, waiting for her horror.

"Kate," she said, and he watched her steely face falter. "Camping?" She paused just a moment and said, "Okay then. Let's go."

While Ty drove, Kate sat half turned in the passenger seat, facing him. He found it unnerving. He glanced over and saw that her eyes were trained on the road.

"Doesn't that hurt your neck?" he asked.

"Pardon?" The windows were open, hot air rushing by. Kate had requested the AC at the start of the trip, but Ty had lied and said he preferred the heat. In reality he just wanted to make her as miserable as possible.

"Your neck," he said. "That looks uncomfortable, the way you're sitting."

He caught Kate squirm. "It's fine."

"You aren't carsick, are you?"

"No…I don't hear very well on my left side." She paused. "It won't affect my ability to do this job," she added, sounding either aggressive or defensive, Ty couldn't pinpoint which.

"No, I'm sure it won't." He smiled to himself. The video camera was designed to rest on the user's right shoulder, and it would render her effectively deaf. Bingo. She was as good as gone.

Three hours later they stepped out of the rental car at the edge of a state park. It was August and Ty wasn't surprised in the least to find so few other vehicles in the parking lot, most of them out-of-staters. An acquaintance he'd consulted had promised that only morons went camping up here during mosquito season. When they'd climbed into the car he'd been pleased to note Kate was wearing a subtle perfume.

She may as well have slathered herself in steak sauce and offered herself up to the bears.

"Here we are," he announced, and the bugs were already finding them.

Kate slapped a fat mosquito from her arm. "Shall I set the tent up?" she asked, fixing him with her eager, go-getter smile.

"I'd like to venture a bit farther into the woods, if you don't mind."

"It's your show, Mr. Tyler."

"Ty. And speaking of shows, I'll need you to carry this," he said, and hoisted a heavy, professional camcorder from the trunk.

"Right," she said with the tiniest pause. He passed it to her and watched her petite frame slump a bit from its heft. "Is it charged?"

"Yes."

"Good. Do you have the manual? I'd like to familiarize myself with it."

Ty frowned with surprise, but he complied and dug the instruction booklet from the car. She made him wait for ten minutes as she slapped the mosquitoes from her face and arms and hair, scanning the pages and toying with the buttons. The bugs were clearly frazzling her, but she looked determined to pretend otherwise. Ty mentally gave her what he imagined was a generous half hour before she cracked.

"All right, I'm ready," Kate announced, standing and shouldering the camera, now down to one swatting hand. "Please speak as loudly as you can if you're addressing me," she added. Her voice had a strange tone in it. Slightly haughty and overly polite. This little hint of vulnerable pride gave Ty pause.

"No worries," he said. "Le's get tramping."

Ty suppressed any feelings of sympathy he was tempted

to entertain during the experiment. He ordered Kate to move here and there, behind him, in front of him, crouching down low, then up high atop a boulder. She tripped over roots and rocks, half-blind behind the eyepiece, at the complete and utter mercy of the bugs. She thrashed occasionally and the bites must have been maddening, but Kate didn't complain. Ty had to hand it to her, she was one stubborn specimen. Strong, too, though he had no doubt she was struggling.

"Okay, that's enough filming for now," he announced after two hours' torture.

"You sure? There's a nice scenic bend just up there," she said, and Ty wondered which one of them was going to surrender first and call the other's bluff. He hadn't counted on her having such a good hand. She knew how to make him sweat. He looked down and saw that the backs of her heels were chafed and bloody.

"Oh, Kate," he groaned, finally using her first name. "Let's just stop, okay?"

She lowered the camera and followed his eyes to her savaged feet. "That's fine—don't worry about that."

"No, that's not fine. Come on, we need to give this up."

"Give what up?" She cocked her head and gave him a calculating look, eyes narrowing.

"You know what. You've proved yourself, okay?"

"So I get the job?"

"No," Ty said with a sigh. He was taken aback when Kate slapped him on the forehead.

"Sorry, mosquito there." She held her blood-streaked fingers up to show him, smirking in a wholly evil way. "Big one."

And that had been it, the first of Kate's many coups. As soon as Ty had acquiesced, Kate had let herself relax into his company. Ty had forced a pair of wool socks on her and promised her the remainder of the three-day trial, one hell of a crash course. The swarms had kept them huddled in the tent for long stretches, and if sharing that tiny space didn't make enemies out of strangers double-quick, they could only have become friends by the time they dragged themselves to his car and drove back to L.A. late that Sunday night. The footage hadn't been half-bad, either.

Ty started back toward the emergency cabin, feeling as though he were carrying a far heftier burden than just the armful of firewood he'd managed to scrounge. He'd just made a decision to gut all of this, these two-plus years of fantastic partnership. But it had been a good run, hadn't it? Of course it had. Kate would calm down. She'd forgive him. Underneath the tough little soldier's body she'd honed these past three seasons, the old Kate was still in there. Behind the practical, mud-caked thermals and jeans, the woman in the tailored blazer was there, her lips still shining with gloss, hair combed and sleek. Kate would remember that woman once they landed back in California, and be glad of a chance to ditch the nastier aspects of production.

"Kate?" He pushed the door in with his boot and found her kneeling on the floor in front of the woodstove, prodding the flames with a stick. She didn't turn, and Ty caught her wiping a sleeve across her cheek.

"Find some decent wood?" she asked, too casually. The sticky quality to her voice confirmed that she'd been crying and Ty felt his heart break. But he knew her. She'd never accept his sympathy, so he'd give her this charade instead.

"Not bad." He let the wood tumble from his arms into a messy pile by the wall and shut the door. "Enough to keep us warm until the morning. Snow's not letting up, though."

"Food?"

He shook his head. "There's nothing out there. What have we got in the pack?"

She turned, finally, and the skin under her eyes was

blotchy even in the dim light. "Not a lot. I just packed some random stuff for my lunch. A bag of cashews, some string cheese and an orange. Sorry."

"Sorry? Do you have any clue how delicious that sounds on day three?" he said, hoping to make her smile.

"Well good, because that's all we've got. And I've got some snow melting in the thermos," she added, pointing to where it sat on the stove.

"Good girl."

She sighed, bitterness peeking through the diplomacy. "Don't patronize me, Tyler."

Ty sighed, collapsed onto the folding chair and rubbed his wind-chapped face. He unlaced his boots and kicked them off, the slushy water sluicing out as one tipped over. He stripped his thick socks off and wrung them out before donning them again, dragging the chair across the room next to Kate and propping his wet feet up in front of the growing fire.

"I'm sorry," he said quietly.

She glanced up. "For patronizing me, or for firing me?"

"I never said I was firing you. Don't be mad, Kate."

"Why on earth not?"

"Don't you miss your regular life, after all this time? Clean clothes? Decent sleep? Hair dryers?"

"I'm not the same person I was when we met, Ty. I like this, okay?" Her eyes burned into his for a moment, unforgiving. She looked back at the stove. "I can't believe you're thinking of doing this."

"I'm not thinking about it. It's done."

"I am so royally pissed off at you." She jabbed at the flames with her stick.

"That's fine with me. I can understand that."

"Just shut up, Ty. Please."

He sighed. "What you said before, about this being your

show, too…you're right. I mean, 'the crew'? It's your name that's listed in the credits for how many other jobs? More than Dom Tyler, even." He ticked her titles off on his fingers. "Additional Camera, Researcher, Travel Liaison, Assistant Film Editor, Mr. Tyler's Assistant, of course. We ought to rename the show.… Maybe to *Kate Somersby: Survive* This *Jackass!*"

Kate didn't reply.

Ty cleared his throat. "You know better than anybody what goes on out here. If the viewers knew how much you really did…well, I'm not all that bloody credible to begin with, but… You could ruin me. In the press, I mean. If you wanted to. Just don't ever think I can't see how hard you work."

She frowned. "Why would I want to discredit you? My reputation's wrapped up in this as much as yours. And we never lied about anything, about the show being simulated, and you having help."

"A hell of a lot of help."

Kate took a noisy breath, sounding exhausted. "Not anymore… You've got to know there's no way I'll keep this job if you take the best part of it away."

"There's still a lot left, Kate. You do about four people's jobs for me, now. There'll still be at least two left for you even with filming gone."

Kate made a disgusted face. "That's like… That's like telling me I can have any part of the lobster except the meat. That offer is like a plate of antennae and eyes and shell parts and a lemon wedge—"

"You're a poet, Kate."

"It's a terrible offer."

Ty didn't attempt to argue further, just stretched his legs out and stared at his feet in their wet socks. "Well, when you get back to town you can exact your revenge," he said, hoping to reclaim some of their old, comforting banter. "You can go run to all the tabloids and tell them what a jerk-off I am, if you fancy. How I hit on you? Sell your exposé to all your beloved gossip rags."

"Shut up." She rubbed her temples as if a headache were overtaking her. "I can't believe you kissed me earlier."

"It was pretty unbelievable," Ty agreed, flirting recklessly.

She kept her eyes on the flames. "Did you decide to do that before or after you chose to ruin my life?"

"About a minute before. So don't worry, it still counts as unwelcome contact in the workplace, if you want to sue me for sexual harassment."

"Don't think for a second that I'm finding you cute right now." Her deadly tone cut him down. She'd always been good at that.

"All right," Ty said, relenting.

They sat quietly for a few minutes, until Ty caught her shivering.

"Your clothes all wet?"

She nodded.

"Mine, too. You know the drill."

He stood but she didn't follow suit. He poked her hip with his toe. "Come on. We've gone this long without anybody catching hypothermia. Let's not ruin our track record now." He yanked the sweater over his head. "Mind you, look what an ironic death did for James Dean."

She rolled her eyes at him but stood, and they both tugged off their damp clothes. Kate stopped at her T-shirt and underwear, holding her jeans up to the stove. She wasn't shy with her body. She had no reason to be—it was fantastic. And anyhow, seeing each other in their underthings wasn't a rare occurrence. Ty stripped all the way down to his boxer briefs and slung his clothes over the folding chair.

Kate kept her eyes on the fire. "You're no James Dean," she finally mumbled.

"Because I don't play the bongos?"

She ignored him.

"Is this weird now, since we…you know?" Ty was dying to bring the topic back around to the kiss.

"Since you forced yourself on me, you mean?" Kate asked, but when her eyes met his he could see a glimmer of her old self in them. Ty rushed heedlessly forward with this tiny poke of encouragement.

"I distinctly remember you letting me."

"I was too shocked to protest," she said.

"I've never seen you shocked before, Kate."

"It's just that I've never been confronted by such a hor-rifying experience before."

"Oh, cheers."

"You remember when I woke up with that huge bat in my hair in the jungle?" she asked. "It was a bit like that, only more grotesque, I suppose."

"It's good to have you back." He smiled at her.

"I'm still pissed," she said, but she sounded tired enough to call a truce, at least temporarily.

"Did you like it?" Ty demanded, unable to dance around the topic any longer. He hoped she couldn't guess how much of his ego was riding on her answer.

Kate didn't reply right away. She turned her jeans the other way around in front of the fire and swiveled her head toward him. Her eyes roamed his body up and down and back again, cold and appraising. He'd never felt so naked before in his entire life.

She looked back to the stove, attention trained on the fire through the open door. "Yeah, it was wonderful."

A flutter of giddy relief upset Ty's stomach. "Oh."

Kate glanced over again. "Happy now?"

"A little," he admitted, unable to keep the corner of his mouth from twitching into the beginnings of a smirk.

KATE CAUGHT TY'S SMILE and returned it, shaking her head with frustrated amusement. Why was it so damned hard to stay pissed at him? She could have managed it, too, if he hadn't brought up the kiss. She'd shunted it to the back of her mind throughout the ensuing fight and the hurried preparations for the shelter. Now it was stampeding to the fore, demanding attention and drowning out her anger.

She glanced at his firelit body, at the six-foot-three-inch mistake she'd been aching to make for she couldn't remember how long. If Kate was about to lose her daily access to this man once they got back to civilization, wasn't this her last chance to slide that one missing piece of their puzzle of a relationship into place? If she was doomed to lose Ty anyhow, she might as well do it right—lose him completely. Boss, partner, friend and finally, perhaps inevitably, lover. She tossed her jeans over his on the chair with a loud sigh of acceptance.

Ty looked wary at first, only his eyes moving as she stepped close and reached out to touch him. Beneath her palms, the skin of his waist felt smooth and firm, and his stomach tensed with held breath. She'd seen the details of his body so many times before, no modesty between them, but now... Now she was allowed to touch. It was like Christmas, this sudden access. His skin was cool on one side, hot on the other from the fire. She breathed him in, eyes locked on his chest.

He reached out to touch her hair, the gesture cautious. "What's on your mind, Katie?"

Staring at his mouth, she felt dizzy, teetering on the razor-thin barrier that had always stood between them. She could knock that final, flimsy wall down now, with just a few little words.… "You can kiss me again."

No hesitation. Warm, firm, full lips rushed down to capture hers, strong hands grasped her shoulders. His mouth was rough and hungry, all the things she felt herself, reflected back in his kiss. Her fingernails dug into his sides. Goddamn, this body…tall and strong, always Kate's territory in every way but this one. As his tongue slipped against hers, tasting her deeply, a streak of desire blushed and hardened between her thighs.

Ty came up for air and stared her dead in the eyes. His own were heavy-lidded now, glassy. "I want you," he said simply.

She liked the helplessness in his expression and the feeling of being the one in control again. "Do you?"

"Yeah. For such a long time, Katie."

"How long?"

His calloused fingers stroked her cheek. "Forever, it seems like. Since the first night I lay next to you in a tent and realized I could sleep because you were there."

"Is that what you want from me right now?" she whispered. "A good night's sleep?"

He huffed a sigh through his nose. "Of course not."

She grazed her fingertips over his stomach, his ribs, his shoulder blades and watched his muscles tense. "What, then?"

"Your hands on me… You feel so good."

"Do I?"

"Don't tease me, Kate. You've got me in pain, my body wants you so much."

She was thrilled at this proclamation. "Your body makes promises that I hope you're prepared to keep," she whispered, hands drifting down to cup the toned ridges of his hips.

"What promises?"

"Ones that keep a girl up at night."

"What keeps you up at night, Kate?"

"You," she admitted with a small laugh, abandoning the taunting. "This," she murmured, and she hooked her fingers inside the waistband of his briefs, pulling them down an inch to reveal the trail of dark hair that led into the intimate shadows below. He was already hardening, his cock straining against the cotton. She licked her lips, suddenly thirsty.

"Just ask me, Kate. I'll give you anything you want."

"Will you, then?" She remembered her beloved job and the thought dulled her pleasure. Maybe she could… No, that was stupid. What did she think this was, a sitcom? A soap opera? Like she could seduce him into signing some kind of contract to reinstate her old job description. Like anyone was *that* sick, using sex to try and manipulate a situation to suit their personal agenda—

Kate's body cooled in an instant, the moment of understanding like a shock. Ty's waistband snapped back against his belly as she yanked her hands away and retreated a pace.

"I know what you're doing," she said. "All this sudden flirting. You're buttering me up."

His brows rose. "For what?"

She aimed her gaze at the flushed skin of his neck, avoiding his eyes. "Because after we wrap this episode and I quit, you know I could go to the tabloids and tell them all sorts of nasty, scandalous lies about you. That's what you were going on about before, isn't it? You were feeling me out, to see if I was going to try and screw you over. Paint you as some kind of incompetent jerk or a fraud."

Ty's eyes widened and his posture slumped. "That's not what I was doing."

"It is," Kate said, feeling as if she'd just put her finger squarely on the crux of the issue. Chemicals flooded her brain and she let anger carry her away from reason and patience and their temporary peace, transforming her into her impulsive, reactionary younger self, the one she'd spent all these years trying to obliterate. Well, screw reason. The old, angry Kate was driving now. "That's why you kissed me to begin with, isn't it? You're trying to make sure I'm on your side. Well I'll tell you something, I've always been on your side. I love this show."

"I never said any of that—"

"I'm not stupid, Ty."

He put his hands to his hips. "No, Kate, but you're doing a bloody brilliant job of playing a paranoid nutcase right now."

"Watch yourself."

"No. You watch it." His body went rigid with anger, an emotion Ty rarely expressed. He advanced a pace, muscles looking tight and fierce. "I never thought any of those things. I'm sorry we can't work together in the field anymore."

"Yeah, right."

He frowned, narrowing his eyes as he studied Kate's face. "And I'm sorry you're making it like this. I want us to be friends when we get back to civilization. I want us to be friends for a long bloody time—"

"Ha!"

"Dammit, listen to yourself, Kate. This isn't you."

She paused long enough to take a deep breath, and to honestly contemplate what he was saying. No, it wasn't her, not the woman she'd worked hard to become—the only version of herself Kate had ever let Ty see. But the pain of what she feared was true had overtaken her senses. The resulting chaos felt good, drowning out the vulnerability and hurt she still felt over losing the best part of her job.

"I never thought any of that," Ty said firmly. "About you running to the papers on me. What have I got to do to prove that, Kate?" He seemed pained by this conversation but determined to find a resolution. Mr. Rise-to-the-Challenge.

Kate grabbed her still-damp jeans off the chair and yanked them up her legs. "Nothing. Just forget it."

She shoved Ty's clothes at him and dragged the chair back to the other end of the shelter, sitting down and picking up the camera from the floor beside her. Turning the power on, she toyed idly with the settings so she wouldn't have to look at Ty. She listened to the fire popping and fabric rustling as he redressed.

"I never thought that," he said again, softer. She glanced at him and his face looked tired, older. "I trust you more than I trust anybody else on the planet, Kate. You've got to know that by now."

She shrugged, bitter. "I don't feel like I know you at all, not after what you've decided."

"I'm sorry it's so upsetting. But I'm not doing it to hurt you. Just the opposite."

Kate entertained a thought that burned in her stomach like acid. "Do you think that accident was my fault? That I didn't prepare us well enough?"

He shook his head and smiled with some sort of discomfort. "No. I've always had faith in your abilities."

She felt her anger resurge. "It sure doesn't feel that way at the moment."

"And you don't seem like the Kate I know, right now. But I do trust you." He fell silent for several minutes and she played with the camera's zoom lens. She popped the cap off and studied Ty's image on the little view screen.

"Everything's always about proving something with you," she grumbled, centering him.

"I'm just trying to—"

"Actually," she cut in, taken by sudden inspiration. "I know of a way."

He blinked. "A way to what?"

"For you to prove you trust me."

Ty stared through the lens at her, expectant. "Brilliant. Tell me. I'll do it."

She adjusted the focus.

"What's on your mind, Katie?" She watched his expression on the viewfinder, curiosity mixed with a growing dose of trepidation.

Kate felt the corner of her mouth curl up with a devilish twitch. "Take your clothes off."

"Beg pardon?"

"You heard me, Ty. Strip. You trust me? Get your clothes off, then."

6

Kate watched Ty blink through the camcorder's screen, his frown demanding a more satisfactory explanation.

"You trust me to go back to the city with this video and everything on it and not sell it to highest tabloid bidder," she said, "and I'll believe what you're saying."

"Of course I trust you not to do that."

"Then prove it."

He stared blankly for a long moment before saying, simply, "All right."

Kate hid her own surely visible surprise behind the camera. She'd never seen him turn down a dare before, but still…

"I don't get it," Ty said, "but tell me what you want me to do, and I'll do it."

"Good." Kate's incurable inner control freak warmed to this turn of events. As she pondered the possibilities, her body warmed, as well. "Take off your clothes again, like before. Everything but your underwear."

Ty complied, in no evident hurry. His sweater and trademark Western button-up were tossed across the bed, leaving just the undershirt that bared his obscenely strong climber's arms. Kate choked down the lump forming in her throat.

The chemicals from her anger mixed with curiosity and nerves, a powerful cocktail brewing in her bloodstream. Ty eased the shirt over his stomach and chest. Kate's breath caught. She'd just seen this, just touched him…but this was different, with her cast as voyeur, not partner. It felt wrong, but backing down would take away the only scrap of control she had left.

Ty's eyes bored through the camera into hers. She felt it then, The Shift. Saw it in the way his muscles tensed and his lips parted. When Ty unbuckled his belt there was an aggression in the gesture, a challenge. He tugged it free as if unfurling a whip and Kate half expected him to advance on her. Instead he folded the worn leather in quarters and tossed it on the floor with a clatter.

He licked his lips. "This is really what you want?"

"Getting there." Kate made her voice as smugly casual as she could manage, hoping the thick weight behind her words would pass for boredom.

Ty unbuttoned and unzipped his pants and let them fall down his legs, revealing the powerful thighs that haunted Kate's dreams, and daydreams. And day-to-day reality. The fire backlighting the scene threw all the contours and shadows of his body into dramatic contrast, and lent a sinister quality to his face. He stepped out of his jeans and kicked them aside. All she'd ever seen of him was before her now, every square inch of bare flesh. Rock climber or not, Ty was built like a swimmer—he had a long, lean, tight body with cresting hip muscles that drew Kate's attention straight between his legs to the bulge in his boxer briefs that she'd flirted with only minutes earlier. Lust banished Kate's misgivings and cemented her determination to see this dare through.

"Now what, Katie?"

She grinned behind the camera. "Touch yourself."

His shoulders slumped and all the cautious amusement drained from his face. "You've got to be joking."

"If you trust me you've got nothing to be afraid of, Ty."

His expression hardened. "I'm not afraid…but for someone who's trying to convince me of her trustworthiness, you sure sound a whole bloody lot like a blackmailer."

"It's your move."

"Fine," Ty said, smiling darkly. "Get comfortable." He seemed prepared to do the same. He grabbed the sleeping bag from the bed and laid it on the floor. As he dropped to his knees, Kate followed him with the camera. The device that had brought them together professionally felt like a shield now. For a few moments Ty did nothing, merely stared her down through the lens. Then slowly his hand snaked across his stomach, dipping beneath his shorts as he adjusted himself. "You sure?"

Mouth dry as chalk, Kate nodded.

He withdrew his hand and cupped it over his bulge.

"Good," she heard herself say, reality fading behind a cloud of dark excitement. She watched him fondle himself, wishing it was her hand touching him, caressing the only bit of him she'd never seen. She'd spent more than one lonely evening imagining such a thing. Her lips twitched, so close to muttering his name.

His touch intensified, the fondling now stroking. She could see him growing, the outline of his erection pressing insistently against the cotton. The muscles of his stomach tightened and swelled alternately with his breathing, tendons standing out in his arm. He stroked the ridge of his cock rougher, making Kate's heart pound with impatience and curiosity.

"Enough?" Ty whispered.

She couldn't be sure if his tone was one of arousal

or anger but right now she didn't give a crap. "Not even close."

"How long have you wanted to see this, Katie?" he asked, turning the tables on her. His hand slipped inside his shorts, again stroking hard.

"This is only to prove a point," she lied.

"I don't believe you."

She swallowed. "That's the point I'm trying to make," she said, only paying partial attention to the argument. He'd met her challenge and was starting to intimidate her. She liked it.

"How long have you wanted this?" His voice turned deep and harsh, hand quickening behind the fabric, taunting her. "From the very start?"

"Show me, Ty."

"Show you what?"

"Show me your cock. Let me see it. Show the camera."

She'd expected further protest, but Ty was done playing. He called her bluff. He tucked his thumbs into his waistband at either hip and pushed his underwear halfway down his thighs, exposing his erection. A charge of fear, hot and thrilling, zapped straight down Kate's spine. His sex looked dark and heavy in the dim, dancing light, and he ran a fist slowly up and down his length, just how Kate would touch it if she could. Her body shuddered with marrow-deep desire.

Ty's breathing was heavy, his lips parted, eyelids looking heavy. "Happy now?"

"Don't stop."

"How far do you want this to go, Katie? You want to watch me come?" His touch slowed, pure torture. "Or maybe you want to help me, instead?" A droplet of clear fluid shone at the tip of his head, then more. He slicked it down his cock.

Kate could feel her core melting, mimicking his example. The camera was unsteady in her hands, every second putting Ty more firmly in control. Yet staring at his body in the firelight, so fierce and ready…for once in her life Kate didn't think she'd mind being the one taking orders. The idea brought a fever to her skin.

"You want to help me, Katie? You want your hands on me? Your mouth? Tell me what you think about. About us. How did you imagine we'd be, together?"

"Keep going," she commanded.

"Put the camera down, Katie."

She held it tighter.

"You've got me so hard it bloody hurts, but I'm not coming until you make me yourself."

The heat and wetness between her legs reached a maddening intensity, demanding she take action. Just paces away knelt the man she'd dreamed about for years, lusted after and also cared for. She'd seen this man ill and injured, strong and unflappable, calm and also racked with mysterious anxieties. In all kinds of weather and in nearly every climate on Earth. The sole part of him that Kate had never before been allowed to lay her eyes or hands on was being offered to her now. Yet she found herself unable to lower the camera for a better look, let alone to stand up and claim it for herself.

"Come on." Ty's hand slowed to long, explicit pulls, teasing her. "Tell me what you think about when you're alone."

"No."

"I'll tell you what I think about."

She wanted to shout, "Yes, yes, tell me!" at the top of her lungs, but her need to stay in control—stay safe—kept her mute.

"I'm so close, Katie."

She managed to mumble, "Keep going, then."

"I want it so bad."

Not half as bad as she did. She felt parched, as if Ty were the only thing that could quench the ache. Her body screamed for her to go to him, to fix this strange transgression, stop being a voyeur, join this man, her partner, and explore every inch of what he was offering. Her mouth was a desert, her hands shaky.

"Last chance, Katie." Ty's arm pumped hard, his hips tensed and eager.

She held her tongue. She was certain that if she tried to speak nothing would come out, anyway. Before her, beyond the camera, Ty was coming undone.

"Oh, Katie..." His head rolled back, the muscles of his chest and abdomen clenched one last time, and then—

Nothing.

He stopped. His hand stilled and even on the tiny digital screen, Kate could make out the trembling of his fingers. After a few panting breaths, he hiked his shorts back up his thighs and over his erection and stood. Kate stood, as well, lowering the camera. She saw him in all the color and intensity of reality again, and the sheen of sweat made his body look at once powerful and desperate. His eyes were lit up bright and hot as the fire. She smelled him, as well—his need. He'd suffused their tiny, shared space with the musk of raw sex.

"I hope you're happy," Ty said, breathless. He barely broke eye contact as he bent down for his jeans and tugged them back on, rethreaded his belt with an air of aggressive finality. He turned and gripped the shelf above the stove with both hands, seeming to fight to regain his composure. Or his dignity.

Kate shivered, too shaken to respond. She set the camera on the card table and clasped her hands to hide their shaking. Across the room, the muscles of Ty's back flexed, and the motion of his ribs told her just how quick his breaths were coming. The rush of conflict and arousal had fled her bloodstream and she felt uncomfortable now, shifty. Her jeans had only half-dried and their dampness made her skin crawl. She got up and dug through the frame pack for her nylon hiking pants and changed into them.

Ty turned around after a couple of minutes' recovery. There was a cocky, threatening quality to his face when he stared at her, and it caught her off guard.

"You hungry, Katie?" It sounded like a double entendre at first, but he passed her to rummage in the pack, split her orange in two with his hunting knife. He handed her the larger half.

"Thanks." She took it distrustfully, holding it in both hands like the spoils of the last couple of hours' strange, tiny war. Or perhaps it was a peace offering. She ran her thumbnail around the inside of the rind, hypnotizing herself with the activity so she could ignore Ty, standing a few feet away with his back to her.

Her body hummed. The throbbing of her pulse extended beyond her throat and heart and wrists—she felt it everywhere. Her eyes darted to the camera, the unassuming black device looking like Pandora's box, a bringer of secrets and truths and the regret that came hot on their heels. She swallowed. The mental image of what Ty had just shown her was indelible. No matter what did or didn't happen from this moment forward, it would stay with her. Haunt her, punish her. It would punish her for not trusting him to begin with, and haunt her with what she'd chosen to miss out on for the sake of her pride and anger.

TY WANDERED TO THE WINDOW to check on the storm. Against the glass the snowflakes tumbled, the biggest he'd ever seen, and he'd seen some serious snow since he'd left Australia. Staring at the flakes whirling in the wind, he tried to zone out, to make his mind go blank so he could begin to get over the ache pounding between his legs and strangling his heart.

Clearly all the time he and Kate had spent pretending to be indifferent to one another's bodies had been building up to this. Only a few short hours ago they'd not even kissed, and now he'd been within a dozen strokes of coming in front of her. On camera. She could be ruthless when she was after something, but what had just gone on was beyond that—a side of Kate Ty hadn't been prepared for.

He did trust her, of course. He'd trusted her with his life without a moment's hesitation countless times in the past couple of years, and he trusted her not to use that video against him, no matter how pissed she might be right now. Ruthless or not, she was a good woman. A good person. Ambitious, no doubt, but not a heartless opportunist by any stretch of the imagination.

It had been an undoubtedly creepy exchange, though, indicative of how desperate they'd become in such a short time, but so painfully different from how they'd always been, as a pair, up until this point.

Ty had been on the opposite end of a camera from Kate hundreds of times, but they'd always been on the same *side*. He didn't like this unexpected new power dynamic one bit. The competitive streak in him wanted to see the conflict through and to emerge the victor, but being pitted against Kate made him sick to his stomach. He wished there was a second chair so he wasn't doomed to stand. He wanted them back on par. He wanted normality restored. He wanted his partner back and he wanted her now, period.

7

"SAY HELLO TO THE VIEWERS at home, Katie."

Kate glanced up from the bed, turning her eyes from the musty deer hunting magazine to the blinking red light where Ty's eye should have been. He was lounging in the folding chair with his legs crossed, camera fixed on her. They hadn't spoken in nearly an hour and the sky outside had grown dark, leaving only the stove for light.

During the silence Kate had calmed, though the image of Ty's naked body and intimate actions seemed burned onto her eyes, lingering like a sunspot wherever she looked.

"So tell me, Katherine Jean Somersby," Ty said in a talk-show tone. "What's the most challenging part of being trapped in a shack in the middle of nowhere with hunky survival show host Dom Tyler?"

"Losing my job," she snarled, trying to ignore him and re-focus on the incredibly boring article she'd been reading.

He lowered the lens. "Kate."

"What?"

"This sucks."

"Yeah, sorry about that. But I'm not the one who landed us in Saskatchewan, if you'll recall. That was your dart."

"You know what I mean," he said. "*This* sucks. Us, like this. Why are we being like this?"

"I'm already sick of this conversation, Ty. There's nothing left for us to say to each other that we didn't cover already."

He set the camera on the rickety card table and walked over to sit beside her, his weight making the bed creak, and sink and tilting her against him.

"I did what you asked," he murmured.

She didn't reply.

"Was that really just a test, Kate? Or did you want that?"

"What do you think?"

"I don't know.… Sometimes I reckon you want that. Like when we kissed, before you freaked out on me. But other times, I don't know… In light of how little time you insist we've got left as partners, I feel like I may as well tell you now that I want it."

She couldn't resist the bait. "Yeah?"

He leaned in close to rest his chin on her shoulder, his mouth very close to her ear. "Yeah."

"For how long?"

"I dunno…forever. And it's gotten worse the longer we've been a team," he said.

"I see."

"I think you feel that way, too, Katie."

"Oh do you?"

"Yeah."

She mustered a small, contemptuous laugh, but her heart wasn't in it.

"Am I right?"

She exhaled. "Yeah, you're right."

He sat up straight, glanced around the cabin as if contemplating the next logical step. "Well," he said, clapping his hands with finality. "We ought to do something about it, then."

Kate raised an eyebrow. "Oh, ought we?"

"Yeah. And no more dodgy power games."

She held her breath as he shifted to face her, cupping a hand over the back of her neck. He turned her head, leaned in and kissed her. A soft kiss, and brief. Heartbreaking. Kate's private synapses had just begun firing again when he pulled away to say, "I know you hate me a little bit right now."

"Yes," she agreed, the word airy and vacant with distraction.

"I know you hate me, but I'm not apologizing for my decision about your job."

Her stomach squirmed.

"Maybe we should treat this experience as a therapy session," Ty went on.

"What do you mean?"

"Would you like to smack me around?"

Kate blinked. "God, that's kinky."

"No, not like that. Unless that's what you're into," he added, the corners of his mouth twitching. "No, just…give me a slap. It might make you feel better."

"That's a stupid idea."

"Go on. Smack me. You did it before and I bet it felt pretty bloody good."

She crossed her arms over her middle. "No."

"C'mon. I dare you. You just watched me beat off an hour ago, for God's sake."

She flinched at his brazen acknowledgment. "Not all the way."

"So let's see your balls, then. I dare you," he repeated.

"That's infantile."

"That's *us,*" Ty said, which was true.

"Fine," she submitted, and before he could respond she slapped him hard—as hard as she had that afternoon—right across the mouth.

"Bloody hell." He grimaced. "I bit my tongue.… Okay, good one. Do it again, now."

"No." Kate tried to keep the angst up but her laughter gave her away and dissolved her combative feelings. Like a hard drink, Ty's proximity wrecked her defenses. He'd always been her favorite vice, and it felt too good when they were like this to let rational thought get in the way.

"Come on," he said. "Leave a mark."

"I'm not hitting you again."

"What are you, chicken?"

"What are you, ten?" she said softly, and gave him the tiniest slap on the cheek. Then another that earned her one of those smiles that melted Kate like a spring thaw. She took his jaw in her hands and kissed him. He let her lead for a few fleeting moments before he tilted his head and deepened it, until Kate felt the forceful glide of his tongue between her lips. She opened herself and let him explore. God, that mouth. She'd lain awake so many nights trying to imagine this.… His palms felt warm and rough on her neck, his voice a low hum full of hunger. The kiss deepened, growing needier and harsher. She hoped the rest of his body would feel this right—raw and gruff and fearless. She hoped she might be about to find out.

She pulled back an inch. "Let me kiss you back."

He complied and Kate got lost in him, tasting and exploring and getting herself drunk on him. She tore her lips from his to kiss his ear, his throat, his collarbone. A low moan rumbled from his chest as she dragged her short nails down his arms. Beneath the thin cotton of his shirt she felt the raised scar on his bicep where she'd given him stitches two years ago. She dragged her tongue along his neck, wanting to memorize this man she knew so intimately in so many ways.

His hands held her shoulders, tight and possessive. "Christ, Kate."

With a swing of her leg she straddled him, tangling her fingers in his messy hair. She felt energy crackling between their faces, saw fire in his eyes. "I wanted to watch you come earlier," she whispered.

Ty smirked. "I wanted to let you.… But that wasn't about us. This—" he said, grabbing her hips and pulling her tight against his waist. "This is us." His mouth crashed down to take hers. "As long as you're touching me," he said against her lips, "I'll do anything you ask."

"Ty," she moaned.

He smiled between kisses. "Did you like watching me?"

She swallowed. "Yeah."

"Good," he whispered. "You don't know how many times I've done that, fantasizing about you."

Pride bloomed hot in her chest. "What were we doing?"

"God, everything. And every time I came, I imagined I was with you. Inside you. That you were begging me to."

She got lost in the fantasy herself for a long moment, got lost in Ty's kisses as she contemplated what the rest of his body could do. She pulled away again to stare at him. "We're going to have sex tonight, aren't we?"

He stroked her hair, studied her face, then broke into a grin. His dimple appeared for the first time since the early morning, the little lines at the edges of his eyes bunching in the way she loved. "Jesus, I hope so. What's your birth control situation?"

She frowned. "MIA. When's the last time you saw me in danger of getting any?"

"Bugger."

"No condoms, then?"

"Nope. After two and a half years, I'd sort of given up hope," he admitted. "What's your time of the month?"

"Pretty safe, but probably not entirely advisable."

"Right…we better decide now to be good, and pray one of us remembers it when things get serious."

She smiled. "Deal. I'll draw up a waiver—"

His mouth took hers, shutting her up. As they kissed, his hands slid up her waist to her breasts, making her light-headed, making sex seem brand-new again.

He broke away to ask, "What do you like, Katie?"

"With you? Anything." She admired his face in the fire-light. His masculine beauty was like a punch in the stomach, knocking the breath from her lungs. And he was infinitely more than a gorgeous face and a body to match.… He was Ty. And he was hers, finally, if briefly.

Her fingers stroked his chin and the stubble of his neglected jaw, enough days' growth that it was soft, not scratchy. She slipped her palm through the gap between his shirt snaps to assess his chest hair—also soft. His breathing turned shallow and when he shifted his hips she could feel how hard he'd grown for her. She conjured the mental image of his cock from earlier, thick and ready, as big and powerful-looking as the rest of his body. Her hands trembled at the thought and she let herself feel small in comparison. For once, knowing she was the weaker one didn't send her scrambling for her invisible armor. In fact, she wanted nothing between them. She fairly ripped his shirt open, frantic with curiosity, needing to feel his naked skin against hers. She shoved his button-up off his shoulders and tugged off his undershirt, then yanked her own top over her head. Before she was even free of it Ty's hands found her breasts again.

"Sweet Jesus, Ty." She got to her feet and stepped back a pace. "Get your jeans off."

He obeyed, standing to ditch his belt and pants. He grabbed her by the waist and turned her around, sitting her down between his spread thighs. His chest was warm and slick, plastered to her back, his erection stiff against her butt. His fingers tugged at the drawstring of her hiking pants. She held her breath, glancing around the shadows of this strange place—

"Oh," Kate said, and it wasn't a sweet nothing.

"What?" His fingers pulled at her waistband, slackening it.

"The camera's still on." Its little red light was blinking, the lens aimed right at them.

"Of course it is," he murmured. "We're documentary makers."

She frowned. "Ty…"

"Don't go getting shy on me now. You still get the footage," he added, his hand sliding into her pants and wrecking her ability to think. As two fingers stroked her through her panties, Kate sent caution scrambling into the corner for cover.

"Yes," he whispered, his fingertips finding the already-hard nub of her clit through the fabric. His free hand cupped her breast, kneading her, then plucking at her nipple through her bra, fingers slipping against the stretchy fabric. Kate's body tightened with desire so powerful it scared her. With his strong arms encircling her, hard thighs flanking her softer ones, his hot breath heating her temple, she felt possessed by him. Controlled. The things she feared most, and right now, the things she craved from him, the one man in the world she did truly trust.

He circled her flashpoint with a cruel thumb, his fingers moving lower to part her.

"Ty."

He moaned, touching her deeper. "You're already wet for me, Katie."

She held his wrist, wanting to be his partner in this exploration, as she'd been in everything else for so long, everything but this. He tugged her bra down to expose her breasts to the crisp air. He took his hand away from her breast to wet his fingertips with his mouth. She gasped as the touch returned, slippery and explicit.

"I want you so much," she mumbled, breath tight in her chest. Two and a half years' worth of longing had flooded her body, making her feel intoxicated.

"I want you, too," he whispered. "Can you feel how much I want you?"

"Yeah." She could feel his cock pulsing against the small of her back with insistence. "How do you like to do it?" she asked, a question she'd speculated about on who-knew-how-many lonely evenings.

"Doesn't matter, as long as it's you," he murmured, a smile in his voice. "You, bossing me around. You can ride me till I'm sore and begging for mercy. Or I can be on top, following every order you want to bark. Hell, we're stranded in the bloody wilderness. Maybe I'll take you hard from behind, like an animal—" He pressed against her, rough.

"Ty."

"Is that what you like? Wait, no... We don't have a mirror, and I need to see you, Katie. Face-to-face." His thumb stroked her faster. "I've waited so long for this. I need to see it, and watch us. I want you to see. I want you to see it, so you'll never forget what my dick looks like, coursing in and out of you."

Kate blushed at his words, crass but exactly what she wanted to hear. The hand teasing her breast snaked down to her lower belly as the other eased inside her panties, his first two fingers slipping against her wet folds. Ty swore, the word swallowed by a groan. "I never guessed you'd feel this good, sweetheart."

His fingers delved deeper, swept over her clit to make it slick then dipped back inside, his thumb picking up its torturous refrain. His chest pushed against her shoulders as he adjusted, angling his arm so he could touch her deeper still.

She moaned. "I want you, Ty."

"I know what you want. I saw how you watched me before."

She nodded.

"Tell me."

"I want your cock."

"Bet you're aching for me now." His fingers taunted. "Tell me."

Kate reveled in his selfish, haughty demands, fascinated by this new side to him. Her boss, actually bossy. "I want you to take me, Ty."

"How long have you wanted that for?"

"God, forever."

He groaned, fingers speeding up. "You're so bloody wet for me." His hips pressed his erection against her, impatient.

"Let me touch you," she said, near pleading.

"Thought you'd never ask, Katie." Ty pulled her body down with his, and she wriggled around so they lay together, chest to chest. He fumbled until her bra clasp opened and she disentangled it from her arms. She ran her hands over his hard chest and belly, dipping them inside his waistband to touch the soft hair where his thigh met his hip, careful to skirt his erection.

"Katie, please."

She grinned at the sudden power reversal. "Please what?"

"Touch me."

She'd been imagining this for so long and now here it was, just seconds and centimeters from becoming a reality. "You sure?"

He swore again, the hand holding her shoulder tightening. "Please."

She slid her hand from his shorts, traced the edge of his cock through the straining cotton with her fingertips. Ty's hips twitched and she could feel him struggling to keep from thrusting, forcing the contact.

After a few seconds' torture, Ty made a soft, strangled noise. "You're bloody cruel."

"We've waited over two years. Surely you can be patient for a little longer?"

"You tease me another minute," he said, "and this long-awaited consummation's happening without you."

Kate grinned, letting him watch her lick her lips as she savored one last moment of anticipation. With sadistic slowness, she ran her palm over his cock.

"Yes."

She cupped him through his underwear, squeezed his length in her small hand. All the teasing left her, replaced with awe. "You're so hard," she breathed.

"This is your fault." He smiled at her in his wicked way, the light from the fire making him look all the more mischievous. He reached between them to push his underwear down, took her hand and wrapped it around his bare flesh, made her feel the smooth, hard heat of his need. She stroked him, cresting her hand over his head and finding the moisture there as his body primed for her. He moaned as she explored, buried his face against her collarbone, suddenly helpless. She heard her name groaned over and over against her neck as she pleasured him.

"I knew you'd be big," she whispered.

He cleared his throat. "Oh? And how did you know that?"

"Because you always were, in my fantasies," she said with a smile, and she heard Ty's distracted laugh, soft against her skin.

"Am I the biggest you've had?" he asked.

"I haven't had you yet."

Ty reached his breaking point. Pulling her hand from him, he pushed Kate onto her back. He shoved his underwear down his legs, knelt and tugged her pants and panties off. Kate gasped as he climbed on top, his powerful arms braced beside her ribs, his knees pushing her own wide. His body always felt huge to her when they hugged, but this took the sensation to a completely new level.

"Oh my God."

"You want this?" he asked.

"I want this," she confirmed, peeking between their bodies. The golden light from the flames painted them in warm, dramatic tones.

The bed creaked as Ty spread his knees wider still, eclipsing the space between them. He reached down and guided his cock to her entrance, tracing his head along her lips and over her clit, bathing her in her own wetness.

Kate shut her eyes and cursed softly with disbelief.

"More?" he asked, circling and teasing. He released his cock to slip his fingers inside her, then stroked his shaft until it shone from the base to the head. Bracing his weight on his hands, he lowered his hips slowly, until Kate felt the slippery head of his cock against her again.

"Ty." She touched his arms, surveying the power there, seeing it in his eyes, feeling it pulsing insistently against her folds.

"I can't wait to be inside you," he groaned. "I want to be a part of you." His hips began to thrust, the ridge of his erection stroking against her in a steady rhythm as he worked to give her this pleasure.

"Now, Ty."

"Yeah?"

"Yeah."

He drew back and used a fist to position himself at her entrance. Sweat was beading on his long torso, and Kate thought the smell of him alone would drive her headlong into insanity. She'd spent years harboring secret fantasies that weren't even half as erotic as the reality he was giving her. She tugged at his hips, desperate. "Come on, Ty. Please."

"I can't say no to that." He pulled back then eased the first inch inside. "Oh, Kate."

She dragged her nails across his skin. "More."

He gave her another two inches, hips moving cautiously. Kate was wet, but he was thick. She felt herself adjusting for him as he gave her more, feeling the faintest discomfort as her body welcomed him.

"Go slow," she whispered, eyes fixed between them, fascinated. This was really happening. He pulled almost all the way out, then surged back in to the same depth. "Now more," she demanded.

They continued the process, inch by delicious inch, until he was buried all the way inside. She wanted to freeze this moment, stay here for a week with her body finally merged with this strong man, her favorite person on the planet. But she felt Ty's desperation mounting.

"Go ahead," she whispered.

"Kate." He pumped his hips, slow at first, growing faster and hungrier by the moment. "You feel so bloody amazing."

"So do you. I knew you would." Her hands roamed up his torso until her fingers tangled in his hair, possessive.

Her hips shifted and they found their common angles and rhythm.

"You're so deep," he moaned. "I can give you all of me."

"Harder, Ty."

He complied, and Kate did as he'd commanded earlier, training her eyes on his cock, sliding in and out of her.

"Watch me," he coaxed.

"I am."

"I've wanted this for so long," he murmured, his tone shifting from frenzied to tender in an instant. "I never knew it'd feel this good."

"I did," she said with a grin, flashing her eyes at his. "I always knew you'd be amazing."

He groaned, pounding her hard for several beats before getting himself under control again. He set them a steady, sensual pace, their union feeling simultaneously sweet and animalistic. Underscoring the primal slapping of his damp, bare flesh against hers, Ty's face was rapturous. Worshipful. As each gorgeous minute elapsed, Kate saw him unraveling, giving himself over to what they were creating together. Then all at once he reeled himself back in.

"Let me make you come, Katie. What do you need?"

"My clit."

He propped himself on one strong arm, his other hand grazing her breast and belly until his fingers fanned out over her mound, thumb circling her clit. Her legs twitched from the shock of his touch.

"Good girl."

"Faster, Ty." Fast like she'd imagined a hundred times, in a hundred motel rooms.

His hips obeyed her.

"Harder." He'd always been rough in those fantasies, burning up for her.

Ty hammered his body into hers, moaning with his mounting excitement, sounding wild, thrilling her. Everything she loved about this man was in full effect, his strength and passion and their undeniable bond.

"Deeper." The word felt disembodied as Kate neared the edge. She stroked his shoulders and neck with frantic hands as the climax swallowed her, sucked her into the whirling energy of their two bodies. As she went under she felt years of longing reach their fevered pitch, a bolt of the purest pleasure she'd ever experienced, so strong it scared her. She heard herself call his name. Then, bliss. She wrapped her arms around his shoulders, legs locking with his hips, wanting to hold him so tight and close they melted into a single person. Reality trickled back in and she felt him throbbing inside her, heard his shallow breathing.

Her brain felt scrambled and she suppressed a strange urge to laugh aloud. "Oh my God."

She let her arms flop to her sides and Ty leaned back. He wore the pleading look of a man in thrall but he smiled down at her, eyes kind behind the desperation.

"Good?" he asked. It was what he always said when he turned to her, sitting on his couch after they'd watched the latest episode of the show airing for the first time on TV.

"The best yet," she offered, her perennial reply. This was normally where they toasted, but there were better ways to celebrate now. She sat up to touch her palm to his face, feeling stunned. She'd never imagined it could be this way between two people. She'd never bothered to hope, never let herself go enough to feel this deeply.

Ty caught her thumb in his mouth, scattering her sentimental thoughts and drawing her back into darker realms. His body shifted, reminding her he had needs of his own.

"You've been such a patient boy."

His mouth released her thumb and she settled back against the small bed, stroking his thighs.

"I can't think of a better way to suffer," Ty murmured. "But we've taken enough chances for one night."

"Yeah, I suppose so." She glanced down one last time, regretful he was about to leave her. When he withdrew she felt empty, in every sense of the word. "What do you need, Ty?"

His voice dripped with an enticing breed of helplessness. "I need to come, sweetheart."

"I thought you might. You've certainly earned it." Seeing this man so frenzied with longing brought out her taunting side. She slipped from under him and stood before the bed. Glancing around, she went to the pack and pulled out a towel, folded it and laid it on the floor.

"Come here." She coaxed him to the edge of the mattress, falling to her knees before him. "Spread those hard thighs, Ty. Let me see what you have for me."

He let her push his legs apart and run her hands up and down his cock, his heated skin still wet from her. He stroked her shoulders and his eyes took everything in. She studied him in the firelight. Ty had the strongest and most commanding body she'd ever touched—perhaps ever seen—and yet he was helpless before her now.

"You look good, Ty." She flicked her tongue over the corner of her mouth.

"God, Kate. Please."

"Please what?" she teased, stroking him.

"Put your mouth on me. Please."

"Mmm…" She smiled up at him one last time then lowered her lips, grazing them over his head. His body hitched with a gasping breath, back arching, more fluid glistening at his tip. His fists grasped the nylon of the sleeping bag beside each of his tensed thighs as she ran her tongue over him, luxuriating in his desperate moans.

"Please, Katie."

She couldn't torture him any longer—she wanted this too badly herself. She'd imagined giving him this too many times to wait another second to make it real. When she took him between her lips, she tasted both of them.

He cursed, body arching again.

She took him deeper, reveling in the feeling of him, thick and hot, filling her mouth. She wrapped her fingers around his base, craving the power that came from being in complete control of his pleasure. She moaned long and low, wanting him to know how much she wanted this, too.

TY WAS LIGHT-HEADED with pleasure. He groaned for Kate in return, tangling his trembling fingers in her hair. His hips shifted, aching for more. "God, Kate."

Between his legs, Kate's mouth was hungry and relentless, exactly how he'd always fantasized she would be. He could feel her energy spiking, that inner control freak in her getting exactly what it loved most. Ty smiled to himself, more than happy to be the one at her mercy. He pushed her hair behind her ears and studied her face, her skin, her lips wrapped around him.

"That's good.... You're so good, sweetheart. Keep going. Show me how much you love it. Show me how thirsty you are for me."

She gave him everything he asked for, sucking him hard, taking him deeper. He felt excitement crackle in his bloodstream when he noticed that familiar red light of the camera blinking at them from the darkness, taking in all of this. His composure waned as the pleasure neared its peak.

"Good girl," he whispered, hoarse. "Keep going.... Make me come." He ran his thumb across her cheek, entranced by the sight of it all. Her hand stroked him once, twice, and Ty was a goner.

His entire body surrendered to his climax, a convulsive, mind-blowing crescendo. His mind went blank as Kate's greedy mouth took his long release, not letting him go until he stilled. For a dozen or more racing breaths he stared down at her; Kate was on her knees, but he was the one rendered utterly helpless.

When she stood he grabbed her around the waist and pulled her into a sweaty hug, wrapping her smaller body inside his, wanting to consume her. He pressed his lips into her hair and tightened his arms around her middle. At this moment, she was his. He already knew that when the inevitable separation came it would be like an amputation, leaving him feeling wounded and incomplete. For now, all he could do was hold fast.

8

FOR THE FIRST TIME Ty could remember, he was happy he couldn't fall asleep. Though emotionally keyed up, he felt supremely content to lie awake with Kate's body tucked against his, to listen to and feel her steady, deep breathing as she dreamed. He was enveloped in a sense of well-being he didn't think he'd ever experienced before, at least not since he was a small child. It wasn't all lovey-dovey, either. He also felt pretty damned smug.

He'd had her. After wanting it for so long and imagining it nearly every night for the past couple of years, he'd finally been able to take her. To please her. To hear her call out his name and feel those familiar hands on him, everywhere... And it had been better than he'd ever guessed. He hoped she felt the same. He hoped he'd been the best she'd ever had, and that any man who came next would have a hell of a time making her forget it. He frowned, considering such an eventuality.

He loathed it when Kate had dates. Her choices...they probably weren't terrible, if Ty looked at them with some degree of objectivity. Which he didn't. Still, no matter how passable Kate's suitors may or may not be, the jealousy was torture—that, and the lack of access. The sudden inability to turn up on her doorstep whenever he pleased, that just about killed him. Lying awake, knowing he'd be able to drop off to sleep again if only he could drive across town and curl up in her platonic sheets and be at peace, then remembering with a start that he couldn't. Because some other man might already be there, possibly doing far more significant things to Kate than disrupting her rest to make her watch bad TV in the dead of night and rub his back until he could relax.

Territorial, that's how she made Ty feel. He held her naked body tighter, thinking about it now. Coming by her place for a coffee and some shoptalk and seeing another man's razor on her bathroom sink… He even thought he could smell the other men. It drove him mad. Made him want to sabotage those dalliances, to leave his own items around her place, to intimidate and undermine Kate's suitors until she was his again, if only by virtue of professional association or time spent together. Sabotage was unnecessary, however—Kate always did the job herself, finding a deal-breaking flaw in her man of the moment and ending things after a month or two. And every time she broke up with one of these men, Ty had toyed with making a move, making their flirtations into something real so he'd stand a chance at never having to live through the jealousy again.

He looked down at her now. Her strong body, soft in all the right places, curled here beside him, content. He grinned. At long last he'd been able to look at her as he came, in reality, not just in his mind's eye. Her mouth and hands and the beautiful, wet heat he'd fantasized about all this time, were all his.

He was going to lose this when they got back home. He was going to lose his access to her, the time, the odd intimacies and this new, fleeting, *actual* intimacy. Ty shivered. But that's all he would lose. He wouldn't lose *her,* not the way he'd feared earlier that day after the sled accident. Never again.

His body tensed around hers, the embrace tightening with possession, but of a different sort than he'd felt before when they'd finally made love. Kate roused.

"Hey." She sounded faraway and dreamy.

"Hey."

She half turned toward him. "Don't tell me you can't sleep after *that?*"

"I don't want to sleep. I might wake up and discover it was all a scandalous dream."

"Nope." She yawned. "That was the real deal. And I'm going to have a sore lady-area tomorrow that will attest to it."

"Poor baby."

"Mmm…" She flopped back against him.

"Kate?"

"Yeah, Ty?"

He swallowed, fear hijacking his pulse. "Is this all we're going to get? Here in this shack in the middle of the Canadian bush?"

She shifted in his arms and made him wait a seconds-long eternity for her reply. "Too soon to tell. But if you insist on gutting my job, then I'm going to milk this last trip for all it's worth."

Ty fell silent, frowning. It wasn't the answer he'd wanted. He'd wanted an emphatic display of Kate's eagerness to continue this indefinitely. And not just the sex—the two of them as so much more than just lovers.

"I wish you wouldn't equate my professional decision with our personal one, Katie."

"And I wish you were better at lazy, postsex chitchat."

Ty frowned. "Seriously, Kate. I need to know where we

stand now. You told me before how much you wanted this, and I thought you meant more than just the sex."

She went rigid against him, her body feeling cold and strangely distant even pressed tight to his. He knew this mood… Kate before she broke up with her hapless man of the month. Well goddamn, Ty must be a new record, getting the brush-off before they'd even been on a date.

"You searching for the flaw that'll give you permission to ditch me?" he asked, wrapping his arms even tighter around her. "I can save you time, you know. For starters, I can't cook, I have a lousy relationship with my parents, I hate getting dressed up… Oh and I ruined your life, apparently. Don't forget that one."

"We can't break up if we're not a couple, Ty."

He freed a hand to touch her hair and sweep a lock of it behind her ear. "Funny, I always thought we were. So do a lot of strangers and most of the women I attempt to date. Half-assed attempts, mind you."

"Lovely," Kate said. "Nothing gets a girl going like a good old half-assed wooing. That's another point against you."

He let her go and sat up. He turned Kate onto her back and got above her, knees and arms braced tight against her thighs and ribs. He held her there, stared right into her face so she couldn't ignore him.

"You want to know why I'm so crap at relationships, Kate? Why I haven't managed to date anyone for more than a month since I moved to the States?"

Her eyes volleyed between each of his and he saw her lips narrow into a defensive line before they parted. "Enlighten me, Ty."

He stared at her, thinking the words. *Because of you.* Because of guilt. Because time and time again, he'd be making love to some perfectly lovely, smart, charming, wicked woman, and then, as he came—Kate. When he was alone at night, when he touched himself—Kate. And he'd have to end it. He couldn't feel good about being with someone if the chemistry wasn't strong enough to banish this woman's smirking face from his mind as he lost himself. And so far, the chemistry had never been strong enough. Not even close.

"Well?"

From her tone alone, Ty knew he wouldn't tell her. Kate was in combat mode, poised to deflect his sincerity and honesty and make him feel like an ass for pouring his heart out. He still believed it was in her, though—a spark like the one he felt, beyond the physical. But he wouldn't get it out of her now.

"Forget it."

Kate sighed and turned her head to the side as if she was ready to go back to sleep. Ty wasn't. If he couldn't break through her armor with words, sex might do the trick. He could guess all he wanted about Kate's feelings, but what went on between their bodies was undeniable.

"We're good together," he said softly, running a hand from her collarbone down between her breasts, over her belly. "In bed."

She met his eyes. "Yeah, we are."

Ty saw her soften a fraction and his chest loosened. "What did that mean to you?" He swallowed, scared of the answer she'd give him.

She stared over his shoulder for a little while, thoughtful and unfocused, before she replied. "It was two people getting what they wanted after a heck of a long wait. If anything, it almost made you ruining my job worth it, okay?"

He pursed his lips. It was a mean retort, a defensive move if he'd ever heard one…but if she was playing that way, she had something to hide. Ty could play that game, too.

"*Almost* made it worth it?" he asked.

"Yeah, almost. It was the hottest sex of my life, Ty, but that job *is* my life, no matter what you say."

He huffed out a breath, frustrated. "Why do you have to be so bloody glib about this? Don't you see how terrifying that was for me, almost losing you?"

Her nostrils flared, Kate's patented, silent version of a withering sigh. "I don't need your protection, Ty. I'm a grown woman. It's the twenty-first century."

"You think I'm patronizing you?"

"I don't think you can help it. You're just one of those men."

His eyebrows shot up. "Beg pardon?" He didn't want to be just any kind of man to her, lumped in with countless others of some uncertain ilk. He wanted to be special, the idiot that he was.

"You're just one of those men who's always got something to prove," she said.

"Am I?" She was right, but that didn't mean she had any right to say it. "What am I trying to prove?"

"Beats me, Ty. But there's something in there." She reached up to tap his chest with her knuckles. "Something that keeps you up nights and doesn't let you relax unless you're in danger of getting your neck broken or your jugular ripped out."

"Just how long have you spent analyzing me?"

"I probably spend a quarter of my time, awake and asleep, within twenty feet of you," she said. "I have opinions. I notice things. I know you."

"Do you?"

"Sure."

Again, she was right. Maybe not the details, but she *got* him. It was maddening. "What do you know about me, Kate?"

"Lots of things."

"Such as?"

Kate glanced around for a moment and shrugged. "I know you wouldn't flinch if a bear charged you, but when somebody calls you by your first name, you grimace like they're raking their nails across a chalkboard."

Ty's heart beat harder and he prayed she wouldn't say it…hearing his first name brought back the worst moment of his whole life in a flash. Almost worse, it brought back the months of hearing his mother saying it, trying to get his attention, to ask him if he was all right, day after day. He swallowed and met Kate's eyes. "Do you reckon you understand me?"

"No," she said. "Not even close. But I *know* you. That's my job. I know your ways, if not the reasons behind them. That's all I've needed to know, as your PA."

"You're not just my PA anymore."

She shrugged again and looked away.

"You're my lover now," Ty said. He got onto his side, pulled her back against his chest and put his mouth close to her ear, his hand on her hip. He felt her body tense against him. "Did you already know how I'd be, before I finally took you?"

"Sure," she said, and her tone was infuriating—apathetic cockiness with no affection underscoring it.

"I see."

"Don't worry—you were better than I'd dreamed. But I knew *how* you'd be, Ty. You're predictable to me now."

"Oh?"

"Sorry. Maybe no one else can even read the language you're written in, *Dominic,* but you're an open book to me."

He flinched, prayed she hadn't felt it. The trap she was setting was one he couldn't help but fall into. She wanted him angry, wanted the upper hand, and she did know him, including how to push his buttons. He moved, releasing her so she came to lie on her stomach on the sleeping bag. Straddling her again, Ty covered her with the length of his body, his arms locked on either side of hers. His pulse quickened from the conflict and the contact in equal measures. Harmless bickering had been their foreplay for two and a half years and for better or worse it still got Ty ludicrously hot.

"Did you know how I'd feel, inside you?" he murmured against her neck.

"Pretty much."

"Did you know how I'd sound?" He felt himself growing heavy and rigid against her bare bottom.

"Yeah."

"Did you know how I'd taste when you finally got your lips around me, Kate?"

She tightened beneath him.

"Did you know how I'd taste?"

"Yes."

Hearing the arousal in her voice, he shifted so she'd feel how hard he'd become. "And I bet you knew I'd make you come first, didn't you?"

"Of course," she said, her cockiness returning in full bloom.

"I can be selfish, too, Katie."

She snorted. "I doubt that."

"Do you?"

She turned her head to meet his eyes. "Yeah. Like I said, it's always about proving something with you."

Damn, if she wasn't going to pay for that. "You don't think I can be selfish?"

"Nope," she said. "With the exception of wrecking my beauty sleep, you always put yourself last. Three days without food and you always wait for me to take a bite first."

"Fine… But I want you right now. Worse than I've ever wanted a steak or a beer."

"And you'll never be able to come until you've gotten me off. In fact, I bet that's the one dare you'd fail at."

"Don't sound so bloody sure."

"I'd put money on it. Go ahead." She rose to her elbows and knees, forcing him to kneel, offering herself. "Show me how greedy you are. Prove me wrong. I dare you."

He glowered at her, but the wager was one he didn't intend to pass up, or lose. With one rough hand he grabbed hold of her slim waist, reaching around and slipping two fingers between her legs with the other to get her ready. He let his fingers glide in and out of her for a minute, rocking her hips with his, listening as her breath grew ragged, studying the shape of her body as it awaited his demands.

"You're already losing, Ty," she said, husky voice betraying her.

"This is all for me, sweetheart. I want you nice and wet for me first—things are going to get rough after I take you."

She made a doubtful noise and Ty upped the speed of the caress. He closed the space between them, brushing the backs of her thighs with the fronts of his, letting his dick rest along the cleft of her sweet, round ass. He bit his tongue, so close to asking if she was ready. It took a concerted effort not to give a damn, but she needn't know that. He drew his hips back and guided himself to that warm, wet, welcoming place.

As he slid in the first inch, she craned her neck, meeting his eyes.

"This is all for me, Katie," he said again, grasping her hips, driving in deeper.

She gasped softly.

"Damn, you know what?" he said, halting his thrusts. He pulled out, leaving her on her hands and knees as he stood from the bed. "Something's missing."

KATE SAT BACK ON HER HAUNCHES, her body humming with impatience as she watched Ty busying himself across the room in the shadows. "What are you doing?"

When he turned back, the little red light came with him.

"God, Ty." She shook her head, pretending to be exasperated.

He smiled at her, wicked, and propped the camera on the mantel above the stove, pointing the lens at the bed, checking the shot in the viewfinder. He came back and joined her, the mattress sinking under his weight. Kate let him push her shoulders back down. He took her roughly again with a loud groan that both thrilled and shocked her. Damn, he was big.

"You feel so good, sweetheart."

Not half as good as you.

His hands clamped tightly around her waist, matching each of his thrusts with a hard tug. "This is all for me, now. But when you get home, it'll be for you, too," he drawled, presumably meaning the video.

"You're hedging your bets," Kate said, voice unsteady from the impact, eager to egg him on. She liked him this way.... When Ty had a point he needed to prove it did something to him, lit something up in his eyes. Too bad she couldn't see them. Behind her he was growing more aggressive by the moment, hammering her hard. She could feel him sliding not just in and out, but against the sensitive skin between her inner thighs, and she reveled in the hard slap of his hips against her backside. She wanted to watch him—his stomach and chest and God, those arms. She craned her neck again for a glimpse of that power.

"You want to see me, sweetheart?" His voice was heavy and dark, sinister.

"Yes."

He grinned, merciless. "Too bad." With a firm hand between her shoulder blades he pushed her down farther, the angle of her body deepening until her elbows slid forward and she had to grasp the metal tubing of the headboard. He wrapped his hands around the fronts of her thighs and pounded himself into her. For the second time, Kate realized how damn good it felt to give up control.

"Ty."

"God, you're wet, Katie. Wet and tight and hot, for me. I only wish I could shoot inside you, sweetheart."

Kate's own excitement mounted with an alarming momentum. "Ty."

"You'd like that, wouldn't you? You wish I could come inside you."

She groaned as he sped up.

"Yeah, you do." Ty stopped abruptly and pulled out. Kate assumed for a second he was coming, but instead he flipped her over to face him. He knelt, and as he wrapped her legs around his waist and rammed himself back inside her, she registered with a primal rush just how strong he was. He sealed them together upright, chest to chest, slippery with sweat.

"Make me come, Katie." His broad hands showed her the motion he wanted from her hips and she obeyed, excited and intimidated by the dark quality in his voice, the glimmer in his eyes, the size of him between her legs. Boss or not, Ty in control was taboo. Letting anyone dominate her like this felt forbidden and darkly thrilling. Kate suspected he was the only man she'd ever allow to be that way with her.

"Faster, sweetheart. Nice and rough."

"Ty."

"Good. Say my name."

"Ty."

"Keep it up. Just like that. I know how much you love to be in charge. Make me feel good, sweetheart. Make me come."

"I will." Her voice had turned shaky and breathless, the dynamic between them like a drug.

"You feel how hard you make me?"

"Yes."

"And how big? Tell me nobody's ever taken you this deep before."

"Ty…" She was in trouble now, in danger of winning their bet. The thrusts he demanded were brushing her clit against his pubic bone, driving her toward climax.

"Why are you getting so tight, Katie?" He drew his head back and stared hard at her, but his hands kept her riding him.

"Ty."

"Don't you dare," he said in threatening whisper, but he was smiling like a madman.

"I'm not."

She was.

"You are," he groaned. He tipped them over, rocking her onto her back and pounding fast and hard, his body dripping sweat, powerful arms braced at her shoulders. Between Kate's legs the dam was crumbling. She couldn't help herself—she reached a hand between them to tease her clit and just like that, she was gone, lost in free fall, crashing into him and finding no respite from his hammering body.

"You cheater," he seethed, but he was unmistakably

triumphant. He ignored her sensitized body's twitches of protest and continued his assault. "You'll pay for that."

"God, Ty—"

"I hope I ruin you for any man who tries to come after me," he hissed, staring her down, thrusts frantic and aggressive.

"You're the only one," she said, sounding maniacal from his impact and the adrenaline and the truth of what she was saying.

"I hope this keeps you up at night. I hope you lose sleep, thinking about this. Look at me," he ordered, and she snapped her eyes to between their bodies, to where his thick cock was surging in and out of her. "I won't let you forget this," he moaned, and she heard his surrender behind the words. Just a handful of beats later he was reduced to grunting, gasping, losing himself. With a groan of disbelief he withdrew, his fist holding his cock tight as he came, his release lashing her belly in long spurts until he finally stilled.

In the wake of passion, as both their bodies relaxed into the relative silence of this remote place, Kate was shocked to realize how much she'd enjoyed what had just happened. And more shocked still to realize she'd orchestrated it herself.

Challenging Ty was like waving a red flag in front of a bull. That was no revelation, but the fact that she'd done it, that she'd intentionally invited him—no, commanded him—to be the one in charge... Well, that was unexpected indeed. She had no doubt that such a phenomenon could never translate over to real life, but the novelty was nonetheless noteworthy. Kate Somersby, happy to be bossed around. Who'd have guessed?

"You. Cheater," Ty mumbled again as he recovered. He

stood from the bed to pull a spare handkerchief from the pack and tossed it in Kate's direction.

"You still win," she said, tidying herself up. "I was wrong."

"Pardon me? You were what?" His chest rose and fell deeply.

"Wrong."

"Well, well…I think that's the first time I've ever heard those words come out of your mouth. Good thing the camera's captured it all for posterity."

"And a better thing that that video is mine," Kate said.

"Bugger, I should have made that the price of the wager. You will invite me over for the world premier screening, won't you?" He switched the camera off and poked a few more branches into the stove to fuel the waning fire.

"Once we get back to L.A., I'm not your assistant anymore," Kate said. "Not on the crappy terms you're offering, anyhow."

"Meaning we can screw anytime we want without it being a conflict of interest?"

"Meaning I'm going to be so unbelievably pissed that you'll be lucky if I return your calls."

"What is with you, anyhow?" Ty asked as he sat, the question sounding like one he'd wanted to pose for a long time. "Why are you like this? Why are you so adamant about everything?" He pulled her down by the shoulders and spooned her, as if holding her hostage in his arms might make her relent. Fat frigging chance.

"I don't know," she said. "I grew up with a lot of siblings and not much money. You have to fight for stuff." She resisted the urge to squirm, to give away any sign of how uncomfortable this topic made her.

"How come I haven't ever met your family? Any of

them? Any of your hundreds of brothers and sisters or your parents?"

"Why would you?" she asked.

"You've met mine."

"Yeah," she said. "Because we did an episode in Australia. You want to do a show about surviving in Boston and maybe you'll meet mine."

"Tell me about yourself, Kate." His voice was soft in her ear. "Tell me something I don't know about you. Something horrible."

"Why should there be something horrible?" She turned her head to meet his eyes.

"Because you talk about your family like they all died in a house fire or something. Like you're an orphan."

"I do not."

"Just tell me something I don't know. Then I'll drop it." He tightened his embrace. "Tell me about your family. I know you've got six brothers and two sisters and you're the youngest. What about your folks?"

She sighed, too exhausted to bother fighting him. "My mom's really tired and my father moved to Florida when I was six."

"You paint a vivid picture."

"What do you want, Ty, a scandal? When I was little my dad ran a shady bar and he took his work home with him. My mom's an angry person and from what I can remember about my dad, they were a perfect match." She paused. "That's it. I'm not close to any of my siblings."

"Are you, like, an emotional orphan or something?"

"Who are you, Dr. Phil, now? People have crappy childhoods all the time. Mine wasn't any more special than anybody else's crappy childhood. Why are you suddenly so desperate to unearth some dark secret?"

"I'm just trying to understand you, that's all."

"Because we're lovers now?" she asked.

"I don't know. Because it might be my last chance, maybe."

"And whose fault is—"

"What did you think of my family?" Ty demanded, interrupting her.

She thought back to their trip to the Sydney suburbs when they'd filmed an episode in the Australian outback. Ty's parents were still married and seemed to live a comfortable but unremarkable life. His father had a distinctly defeated quality to him, a zombieish, chronic depressive kind of aura. His mother oozed the cheerful, desperate optimism of a woman who was trying very hard to compensate for her despondent husband, but who probably felt equally lost.

"Your parents are very…different from you," Kate concluded. "And each other. And your brother's even weirder." Ty's older brother was in banking in some vague, titled capacity, and he had a wife who looked as if she'd been selected with the same strategic scrutiny as his BMW or Italian shoes. Even his haircut looked as though it had a stick shoved up its ass. He and Ty were similar enough physically that Kate had been left with an impression of two twins separated at birth—one raised in the boardroom of a Fortune 500 company and the other in a tree.

"Did meeting them shed any light on me?" he asked.

"I'm not interested in analyzing people, Ty. That's why I moved to L.A. I'm quite happy judging books by their covers." A half-truth. Kate had little patience for hidden agendas, but of course she was curious about the naked man currently wrapped around her. Still, she valued privacy over understanding. Intimacy was a two-way street, and she didn't much care to be that open, even with Ty. *Especially* with Ty. He routinely made her feel raw and exposed, by virtue of their lingering flirtation. Whether he knew it or not, he had plenty of ammunition already. She had no idea why he seemed so eager for her to have the same arsenal.

Behind her, Ty grew restless. He slid a thigh between hers, making her breath catch. A warm, rough hand ran over her ribs and cupped her breast, and his voice was close behind her good ear.

"Have you ever been in love, Kate?"

Her body gave a little jolt, giving away her surprise at the question. "In retrospect, no."

"So you thought you were, at some point." He nuzzled her neck and shifted, and she felt him, hard against her bottom again.

"Have I told you you're really lousy at pillow talk, Ty?"

"Tell me." His hand left her breast to slip down across her belly, his thigh driving farther between her own to widen them.

"Fine. If you must know, I was engaged before I moved out to L.A."

"Aha."

"And I was ditched at the altar."

"Really?" His hand paused, millimeters from her clit.

"Well, I was stood up at City Hall, yeah. Happy now?"

"Wow." He was silent for a minute, contemplating this informational coup. "So let me guess—"

"Jesus, give it a rest."

He plowed onward. "After you were left humiliated at the altar by your betrothed, you ran away to the West Coast, determined to prove yourself and get your revenge by being wildly successful, while also vowing never to trust another man with your heart again?"

"No, Ty."

"Oh."

She rolled her eyes. "No one's that trite."

"So what, then?"

She exhaled, resigning herself, eager to get this over with now that Ty's strong, ready body was transforming her immediate priorities. "I got dumped on my wedding day and it was the best thing that could have happened to me. That guy…good God."

"Loser?"

"No, he was fine, I guess." She smiled, shaking her head. "Poor thing. Thank goodness he found the balls to stand up to me, because it would have been a disaster. I basically bullied him into proposing so I'd have an excuse to get the hell away from my hometown and my stupid waitressing job and my whole deadbeat family. When he didn't turn up I hocked the ring and drove cross-country so I could find some celebrity who wanted to pay a control freak like me to run their lives. So you're wrong on all counts."

"So essentially, you left your fiancé for me?"

"Sure, Ty. If that makes you feel like a big man, sure. I've found our symbiosis very satisfying. Mystery solved."

"So I'm just the sort of mess you were hoping for?"

"I didn't want a mess. I just wanted…" She wasn't sure how to end the statement.

"You need to be needed?"

"Sure, Peter Gabriel."

Ty ignored her comment and rolled her onto her back, straddling her. "And now you feel like I don't need you anymore so you hate me? Has my decision emasculated you?"

"No, but if I had a dick you'd be withering it with all this Freudian psychobabble bull," Kate said.

"Fine, I'll leave it then."

"What a good idea—"

"But I *do* need you," he said.

"Well, you better get your needs met while you still can." She ran her eyes from his face down his long, powerful, firelit body, to his cock, hovering erect above her navel. Kate memorized him, knowing this was an image she'd be loath to let fade once they managed to get back to their day-to-day lives.

Above her, Ty looked thoughtful. He ran a hand absently over his skin, from his hip to his thigh. The gesture was a potent reminder of how he'd looked earlier, during their strange on-camera standoff. She crossed her arms behind her head to indicate she expected another good show.

"Tell me, Ty…"

"Mmm?"

"Now that you've finally had me, has your itch been scratched?"

He offered her a slow, lazy smile and shook his head. "No. It'll be way worse now."

"Oh?"

He nodded and the hand grazing his skin crossed over his hard stomach to stroke his erection. "Now that I know how good we are together, I'm ruined."

It was Kate's turn to smile. She was uneasy about continuing this flirtation, about relinquishing any power to him by letting him know how much it had meant to her. But their bond was impossible to resist at moments like this. Watching his fist running up and down his cock, his body a playground of bare flesh just waiting to be used and enjoyed and made to beg for mercy… Her own body wouldn't allow her to pretend indifference. She stared at him with shameless fascination.

"There's going to be some mighty lonely nights waiting for us back in L.A.," Ty said, his voice quiet, low and taunting.

"I'll have my memories."

"So will I."

"And my video."

"And you know where I'll be all those nights. Just a twelve-minute drive from you, doing this." He glanced down between his legs. "Thinking about what we've found here, together. What we've done. And I'm going to pray every bloody night that I'll hear your key in my lock, telling me you've come over to join me."

"Ty." Even Kate didn't know if she was trying to discourage him or just the opposite.

"Do you want to know what I think about the most, sweetheart?" he asked, his face taking on that glazed look of aroused distraction.

"What?"

"Your office, that corner of your living room with your desk and your files and that chair you paid like two hundred bucks for and I said it was mad."

"Yeah."

"I think about you, in a skirt, in that stupid overpriced chair, and me on my knees in front of it, and your legs wrapped around my ears while I taste you."

Kate's core spasmed. She swallowed. "And what am I doing, in this fantasy?"

"Oh, you're just ignoring me. Or pretending to. Making your endless phone calls, updating the website…but you slowly come undone with every lap from my tongue until I feel your hand on the back of my head, taking control."

"How perfectly apropos." Kate had spent plenty of hours ignoring Ty while he lazed around her living room, reading her gossipy women's magazines, amusing himself while she finished with business so they could go out for dinner or a drink. "Is that what you've been thinking about all those times I kept you waiting?"

He just smiled.

"You're a very bad man."

His hand quickened. "Tell me you thought about me, too."

"I did," she admitted. She freed one hand from behind her head, and slid it between their bodies. Crooking a finger, she ran it over the soft skin of Ty's inner thigh. She dragged it slowly across his balls a few times before she cupped him, eliciting an involuntary thrust that made the powerful muscles of his hips and abdomen stand out in the flickering shadows of the firelight.

"Tell me, Katie. I want to know what you'll be thinking about when we get back, all those lonely nights."

Her heart beat hard against her ribs, but more than she feared giving up some power and admitting her feelings, she wanted to share them. Just a bit, a taste of how she really felt behind the stubborn facade. She held his eyes. "I always just fantasized about us finally giving in, after all that time. Just in my bed, or a motel bed, or a tent. Just you and me, discovering each other."

He shifted now, moving his knees between hers and slipping inside her like they'd been doing this for years. His voice turned heavy and dark. "And now what will you think about? Now that we've given in?"

Kate toyed with being cruel and dismissive, but thought better of it. "Now I know what you look like, Ty. And how good you are. I'll just relive what's gone on, here in this place." She glanced around the shack, their unexpected honeymoon suite—the place where they had both finally surrendered.

"Good." He slid in and out of her, smooth and slow. "I'll be so close. You could always come over, and let me give you more. Let me give you whatever you can dream of."

"You know we—"

A terrifying blast shattered the peace, and Kate watched Ty's face contort with horror, illuminated by a sudden orange flash.

9

K ate jerked her head back to see what had caused the explosion of noise and light.

"Oh my God!"

White smoke billowed into the small cabin as flames licked through a burst seam in the woodstove's chimney. A foot from the ceiling, the metal chute glowed bright, angry red.

They tumbled from the bed and Kate was racked by convulsive coughs as the smoke closed in on them. She doubled over and felt Ty grasp her by the upper arms. He rushed her to the door and yanked it open, shoving her out into the driving snow and the damp, permeating cold, the blessed clear air. Icy slush enveloped her bare feet to the ankles. Heavy wet flakes whipped her naked body and obscured her vision as the gusting wind stripped all the heat from her skin. An almighty cough forced the smoke from her lungs and she found her voice.

"Ty, get the camera!"

He'd gone back inside and she couldn't tell if he'd heard her. She rubbed her sternum, chest tight from the freezing air and the smoke and the fear. Amid the sounds of the fire she heard glass break and smoke billowed from the little side window.

"Ty?"

Things flew from the cabin—the sleeping bag, their clothes. Ty's boot soared through the door and struck her hard in the shin. She backed up a few paces, feet prickling from the icy soup underfoot. More items followed—the pack, more clothes, then finally Ty's tall form, a firelit vision of bare muscle, obediently lugging the camera.

"Here!" he shouted, his voice hoarse as he dropped the equipment at her feet with a wet thump. "Here's your bloody camera!"

He turned to root around in the strewn items, finding his jeans and pulling them on, then his shirt. Kate followed suit, finding all of her clothes save one sock. Flames burned bright from the chimney, illuminating the bizarre scene. She glanced over at Ty tugging his boots over bare feet that were surely as wet and aching as her own. His actions seemed jerky and agitated, made more frantic by the chaotic, dancing light. She stepped to him, picking up her hat as she approached.

"Holy crap," she said, tugging it on. "That was messed up."

"Messed up? *That* was messed up?" His eyes snapped back and forth between hers, making him look crazy. His head snapped to one side, as if an invisible hand had slapped the sense back into him. The manic energy left him, as quickly as it had come.

Kate shivered in her wet clothes. They still had at least three hours before sunrise.

"We've got to get dry," she said, and Ty nodded. She grabbed the camera and followed him to the opposite side of the cabin, upwind from the smoke and flames. The blaze had spread to the roof, though the snow seemed to be dampening it. They stood as close to the fire as they dared, but with its heat whipped away by the winds, it was useless for drying their clothes. Kate's panic grew as her violent shivers deepened. Her teeth chattered.

"Jesus, Ty, what do we do?" Recent sexual phenomena aside, she couldn't remember ever putting him in charge off camera before now.

"We let the fire burn itself out." He sounded remarkably calm. "Film it." He nodded at the camera bag by their feet, his tone difficult to interpret. "I know that's what you want."

Kate obeyed, unsure of what else to do. She hoisted the camera and switched it to night vision, trained it on Ty's face.

"Well," he began. "I'm tempted to use a different word, but I'm sure they'll just bleep it out in editing. This is massively effed up." Ty turned away to stare at the burning cabin and Kate took it in with the lens. He faced forward again. "It's about…I don't know, three in the morning, maybe, and I think what we're looking at is a creosote fire. I've never seen one in person before, but when I turned to look up at the metal chimney of the woodstove a few minutes ago, while the crew and I were camped out peacefully right inside there, it was glowing bright orange. Molten hot. It split open along a seam and the rest is history." He shrugged, looking dumbfounded. "As you can probably tell, the storm's still going great guns, and we're pretty soaked. It's so furious I can't imagine making any kind of snow den now without risking our necks with hypothermia. If I can, I want to see if these flames die down and maybe try and make a lean-to with whatever's left. Maybe knock the bad bit off the chimney and at least get a little fire going again. Fire's key. We're in serious trouble here if we can't get warm and dry as soon as possible…."

He trailed off, turning away, and Kate joined him in watching the shelter that had finally brought them together as lovers crumble down to smoking ash.

Ty caught Kate's eye and shook his head. "Turn it off." As soon as she cut the power he dropped to his knees, clutching his head in his hands. A sound like an animal being choked issued from deep inside him.

"Ty." Kate crouched and put a hand on his back. He was either retching or sobbing, she couldn't tell which. She ignored her stinging feet and rubbed his back for a few minutes. Eventually his breathing slowed and he stood, looking slightly more like his usual confident self. He offered no explanation for the breakdown.

For a long while they stared at the cabin in silence. The roof was still burning but the smoke had thinned and the fire seemed to be losing its fight with the snow. Kate felt thankful for the moldy wood. If this thing had been new it probably would have gone up in a heartbeat. As the flames died, so did their light.

Ty trudged a few paces to rummage through Kate's frame pack. "Is there a torch in here?"

"Yeah, there should be. Front pocket."

He found the flashlight and switched it on, training the beam around them.

"It's looking pretty solid," Kate offered, and as she said it there was a great creaking sound. In a rush of snow and ash, the roof caved in on the cabin. "Oh."

"Jinx," he murmured, and she knew the old Ty had returned to her.

A few minutes later he ventured inside the shell of the softly smoking former shelter and returned with the folding chair. He set it beside Kate in the snow. When she sat down it sank four inches into the slushy mess.

"How are your feet?" he asked.

"They're tingly. And not in a good way."

"You find socks?"

"One."

"That's one more than I found. Let this be a lesson to the viewers at home."

"What? Don't fling your clothes around willy-nilly when you're having a tryst in an emergency cabin with an old chimney?"

He nodded, looking hesitant but amused.

"This trip is not going as smoothly as I'd envisioned," Kate sighed, staring into the dark woods. "There was nothing about a blizzard or a sled wreck or a creosote fire in my itinerary."

She felt Ty's hand alight on her hat. "Anything else you'd like to add to that list?"

"You're speaking of my being savaged by a wild animal, I assume?"

His fingers drummed the crown of her head.

"Yes, that was unexpected, as well. As were…other things." She didn't want to completely open the wound of being forced off the best part of the show, plus seeing Ty so upset held her back from starting another argument.

"I'm going back in," he said.

She said nothing, just watched his back as he walked away from her.

TY LEFT KATE AND APPROACHED the shelter with the torch. He stood in the doorway and swung the beam around, searching for errant fires, listening for ominous creaks. "Looks safe-ish," he shouted behind him. "But hang back, let me be sure."

He pressed a palm against one of the walls and it felt cool enough. He was being impatient and probably pushing things beyond what was strictly advisable, but goddamn, it was cold. They needed fire. He was too underrested and too underfed to bother being cautious. This entire trip seemed doomed, anyhow. He suspected karma was driving this disaster, finally ready to collect on his old debts. Fine if it were only his neck on the line. That Kate was involved was deeply troubling. More troubling than the cold or the damp or the danger.

Ty walked all around the cabin, pressing on the walls to see how sturdy they were. Somewhat assured, he crept inside, over the floor now strewn with wet, scalded roof shingles and burned beams. Kate's lighter had been sitting on the shelf before the explosion and Ty found it beside the stove, reduced to a lump of molten plastic. He found the axe, as well, blackened but otherwise unscathed. It was warm to the touch, but not hot. He picked it up, pausing a moment before raising it over his shoulder and swinging it against the split in the stove's now-freestanding chimney. With two whacks it broke off completely, clattering to the debris-cluttered floor. Ty gave it a kick for good measure, just as he heard Kate's cautious footsteps behind him in the rubble.

"Your lighter's buggered," he said. "You have any tinder?" He heard her moving, the zipper swishing open on the pack. He used the axe to break the burned-out back wall of the cabin open farther, prying off the blackened edges of the boards and tossing a pile of them next to the stove. He rummaged in his pockets and was surprised to find his flint stick still where it always was. It seemed unthinkable that anything should be so dependable at this moment.

"Here." Kate held out a strip of cotton gauze from the first aid kit she always packed and he took it. Authenticity could kiss Ty's ass right now.

Soon there was a small fire burning innocently in the belly of the stove that had started all this drama. Ty cleaned his sooty hands with a palmful of snow and wiped them on his jeans.

"Good work," Kate said.

He swiveled his head to look at her. Standing beside him, she looked rumpled but calm, and he could feel his heart aching as though some unseen fist were trying to squeeze the life from it. He put his hands on either side of Kate's head and brought his own down to it, mashing her forehead hard against his lips and holding her there.

"Ow, Ty."

He ignored her protest, held her tighter.

"You're hurting me."

Well, at least that proved he hadn't killed her. He pressed his lips against her skin for one last breath and released her.

Kate pointed at the stove's fresh fire, flickering away. "How about that? Premade char wood."

It was odd, looking at her now. An hour ago they'd been in this same space, making love by the light of this stove. Now they stood on the remains of the roof, thick flakes of snow and ash flurrying around them like gloomy confetti.

"Wind's not too bad," she said. "We could use some cover, though. What do you think?"

"I think you should go bring that chair back inside and put your feet up by the fire. I want to get you back to L.A. with all your toes."

"Fine."

As Kate followed his orders—a change in itself—Ty went to work on the wood. He gathered all the old beams that had formerly held the roof up and got them ready for the fire. A makeshift lean-to would be tough. Hacking apart any of the walls might cause the entire place to collapse. Instead he took the axe to the door hinges and splintered it free, then dug the bed out from under the snow and debris and tossed the useless, half-burned mattress aside. He replaced it with the door, creating a sort of platform over which he spread the sleeping bag—melted at one corner but otherwise fine. He dragged the assemblage close to the fire, kicking Kate out of her prime foot-drying space.

"I've seen the marriage bed looking better," she said, joining him in sitting on the door-turned-table, huddling close to the stove.

"I'm sorry about all this," Ty said, wanting to put his arm around her, but feeling so utterly cursed right now he was scared to touch her.

"It's not your fault. It's not like we had time to check for creosote buildup in the middle of a blizzard."

"It's my show. You're here because of me."

"Yeah, I am," she said, her voice soft.

"I don't know why you like this job," he said with a sigh. He watched her, the fat snowflakes gathering on her hat then melting and dripping onto her lap.

"Why wouldn't I?" Her eyes looked black in the dim light, and shiny like glass. "It's like the coolest job ever. And I have a good life insurance policy."

He stared at her, hard. "That's not funny. Do you get why I can't let you do this anymore?"

"Yeah, and you're completely wrong. And I *will* talk you out of it by the time we get back to civilization."

He shook his head.

"We'll see. I just wish you could grasp how ridiculous it is, you thinking something's too dangerous. I've seen your climbing videos. You've got no right to tell people they're risking too much."

He shook his head. "That's different. That's only my neck on the line. I can't let you get hurt doing something for me."

"It's not just for you. I love our show."

Ty stared at the flames. "I know you do."

"Sometimes I think I love it more than you do," she said.

"Doesn't that strike you as a bit unhealthy, Kate?"

"Nope." She fiddled with the hem of her pants for a moment. "I like having something to call my own."

"You should get a dog."

She fixed him with unamused eyes. "And you should wear a harness when you climb. But neither of us is going to change. I'll always be a control freak, and you'll always have a death wish. I'll drop dead of a stress-related heart attack at fifty and you'll finally meet your end at the bottom of some crevasse. But if either of us had to change tomorrow, we'd be dead the day after."

Ty didn't reply, his eyes leaving her face to watch the fire.

"People don't change," Kate said in conclusion.

"Yeah, they do. If something else matters enough."

"Well, I've never met anybody who changed for the better. At least not permanently. Trust me. I've got eight siblings who've never even managed to make it twenty miles from their hometown, who still get up to all the same bull they did in high school, with all the same people."

"You changed, didn't you?"

She shrugged. "The only difference between me ten years ago and me now is that nobody can tell I'm white trash anymore. Not without doing some digging. But I'm still the same person."

"What was your life centered around before this silly show?"

Her gaze darted to one side, irritated. "Don't call it silly."

"Fine. This amazingly useful and benevolent program that's surely saved thousands of lives. What came before this?"

"Well…"

"Come on," he coaxed.

Her lips pursed and Ty knew she was suppressing a smile. She'd worn that face with him a thousand times, the one that usually told him she was trying very hard to not find him clever. "It'll seem really stupid," she muttered.

"How much you care about this show will seem really stupid in five years. Go on. We've had sex, now, in case you didn't notice. Don't try and act like we're not as close as we both know we are."

She fidgeted, seeming nervous. "Well, I used to be su-perobsessed with celebrities."

Ty nodded, not surprised. She might be the picture of practicality when they were filming, but Kate loved all that red-carpet crap. "Like who?"

"Oh, it didn't matter who. I was a total magazine junkie, like fashion and gossip and lifestyle stuff. Before reality TV took off and everybody had their own show and you had to see how totally boring they are outside of scripts and sound bites."

Ty smiled, pondering this. "All right. Go on."

"I grew up so poor, the ridiculousness of the lifestyles was, like, mind-blowing." Talking about this, Kate sounded ten years younger. Animated. Ty liked it.

"I didn't want to live that way," she said. "Not really, but I dunno…it seemed like some crazy other world. An alternate universe to where I was doomed to be. Like reading about some kind of made-up fantastic creatures. I knew I'd never *be* that, but it seemed so exotic. And fascinating."

"Sorry you ended up with me."

"Like it or not, Dom Tyler, you are an up-and-coming celebrity. You've been in *People,* you know."

"Have I?"

"Yeah, plenty. You'll probably be featured in the 'Sexiest Man Alive' issue this year. You'd know that if you ever looked through the clippings binder I keep on my desk. And you've been in *Parade*, and on *ET,* and Ellen DeGeneres has talked about you on her show, a couple of times. *Esquire* wanted to do that little piece that you turned down because you were convinced they'd make you style your hair like some 'new lad' or whatever you called it. You'll be properly famous in a couple more years. You're already properly famous in Australia."

"I'm no Mel Gibson."

She smirked. "Thank goodness. But you *are* famous. You're a heartthrob," she said, smiling and poking him in the shoulder.

Ty made a disgusted face. "Standards are really slipping."

"So anyway, I got my wish, Ty. You're my celebrity."

"That just means I'll be washed up in a couple more years, begging to be on one of those D-list dancing shows. I do hope you'll tune in, Kate," he said, glib. "You should be the famous one, you know. You're a hell of a lot more capable and charming than me. And you're hot."

"Yeah, right."

It was his turn to shrug. "You don't give yourself proper credit. You're enough on your own, without needing somebody less competent hanging on to you for dear life. And I'm good at hanging on to things—it used to be my job. I won't need you forever, Katie. You should be working this hard for yourself, not somebody else."

Kate looked down at her feet for a long time, not responding, and Ty let it drop.

"Snow's letting up, I think." He squinted skyward. The flakes were smaller and fewer now and the wind had diminished.

Kate glanced up to confirm. "What should we do?"

"Wait till it's light. Try and get a signal fire going if the visibility improves. If it doesn't, maybe keep following the trail. Fishing shelter's got to be walkable by now. What, maybe ten miles?" he asked.

"Hard to say. I lost track of the distance when we were on the sled. Could be closer. Could be farther. Plus we've yet to hit the fork." Kate pursed her lips. "We won't be able to tell which way the dogs went, now, but even if we take the wrong one, at least we'll be closer. Maybe we could signal, then, if the clouds thin."

"Yeah. Well, we'll live. That's the important thing."

Kate nodded. "It'd be embarrassing for a survival expert to die on the job."

"What would the tabloids say?"

"I dunno, but I'm sure there'd be a TV movie about it," she said.

Ty laughed. "Lovely. If you make it back to civilization, I give you permission to do the casting, and to have an illicit affair with the bloke playing me."

She smiled and shook her head. "I'm sure it would pale in comparison to the real thing."

Beneath the pleasure of seeing Kate smiling, Ty felt bitterness surfacing. He couldn't help but wonder which she cared about more—him, or the show. The show or herself, for that matter. Her priorities baffled him. That she'd called out in concern for the bloody camera as their shelter erupted in flames, as if it were her child, for heaven's sake. Damn, that had hurt.

"What will you miss more, Katie, when this is all over? Me or the show?"

Her mouth twitched as she considered her response. "It doesn't matter, Ty. By the time we get back, I'll still get both."

A COUPLE HOURS LATER the snow had officially dropped to picturesque, Christmas card proportions. Visibility was poor, but the sky was beginning to lighten with the approaching dawn. Kate glanced down at Ty, lying awkwardly on his back with his legs dangling off the door-bed, fingers linked atop his chest.

She'd spent nearly the entire time since their conversation had dried up thinking about the last thing he'd said. Of course she cared more about him than the show. Looking at him now, it was hard to imagine her day-to-day life without him. Still, not seeing him at all would be easier than seeing him in L.A., then saying goodbye when he left her behind for months at a time to do the part of the process she'd come to love most.

She tapped his shoulder. "Hey. Ty."

His eyes opened with a swiftness that told her he'd been awake this entire time. "Good morning, sunshine."

"Exactly—it's getting light. And I'm getting sick of just sitting here."

He squinted into the open sky above them. "Not looking too promising for a signal fire, is it? What do you fancy? Up for a hike?"

"Yeah, sure. If it's unworkably bad we can always come back and wait. But I can't imagine you want to sit around doing nothing, either."

"And I bet you're just dying to get all this on film, aren't you? Next week on *Survive This!,* Dom Tyler actually survives something." He held his hands up as if he were envisioning the ad. "Let me try and find my socks."

"I'll help." Together they sifted through the slush and shingles until they'd recovered Ty's two missing wool socks and her single one. She draped them over the stove to dry and they sat back down on the door.

Ty laughed to himself.

"What?" Kate asked, looking over with a skeptical smile.

"We had sex," he whispered, conspiratorial.

She rolled her eyes. "Well spotted."

"When the season three DVD is released, I'm thinking it'd make a great bonus feature."

Kate slugged him hard on the arm, pretending to be merely mock-irritated, but feeling genuinely angry. She was still tender from their lovemaking, both physically and emotionally, and she didn't want it spoken of so lightly. The rush of vulnerability made her shiver and in its wake she felt resentful. "Don't tease me about that video. *My* video."

"Are you worried that if it got out, everyone would see your tattoo?" Ty asked.

Her eyes narrowed to slits and her shoulders bunched up reflexively at the comment. Kate hated her tattoo. Her "tramp stamp," as they had since become known. A Celtic design across the small of her back had seemed like a great idea when she was a rebellious seventeen-year-old, but now it was her dearest wish to get it removed as soon as possible. The final erasure of all the evidence of her former incarnation… Just a couple hundred more bucks to go and she'd have the money saved up. She glared at Ty. That was a low blow and he knew it.

"Don't look so pissed," he said. "It's cute."

"Let's get a move on," she said, anger bubbling.

"You're the boss." God, same old Ty. That glimmer of him she thought she'd seen when they'd been intimate must've been a trick of the firelight.

They pulled their hot socks on and their boots, and Kate did her best to organize the pack.

"Hey, Katie."

"What?" She didn't bother glancing up from her task.

"Look at me."

She complied, meeting his eyes in the weak morning light. "Yeah?"

"Stand up straight."

"Why?"

"Because I bloody want to kiss you, that's why."

She stubbornly turned her attention back to the pack.

He made a little *hmm* sound, clearly amused. "Are you mad at me?"

"I'm just trying to be professional, Ty. You ought to try it sometime."

"You don't want to kiss, then? One last time before we leave our love nest?" She could see him in her periphery, waving his hands to encapsulate the smoke-stinking remains of the cabin. Her cheeks burned. She stood and shoved the pack into Ty's arms, then walked away from him, grabbing the axe and heading toward the route they'd been following when they'd found this place, what felt like a lifetime ago.

The ground was even worse than when they'd been tossed from the sled. The storm had added at least a couple inches of slush to the frigid stew underfoot, and Kate gave them a generous two hours before their so-called waterproof boots began to fail. Still, this was better. She couldn't sit back there anymore, not next to Ty. Not now that his feelings about the previous evening's events seemed to be coming clear. She was relieved she hadn't given away what it had really meant to her, apart from red-hot sex.

"You want to film me?" Ty asked, sounding uncharacteristically soft. She didn't blame him. He'd gotten no rest in the past thirty hours and hadn't eaten a real meal in three days. She forgot sometimes what he put himself through for this. As much as she did. More. Maybe he was right. Maybe he didn't need her, after all.

A long, loaded breath oozed out of her. "If you're up for it, yeah. I'll film it."

"Sure."

Kate traded him the axe for the camera and got herself equipped. "Rolling."

"Welcome to day four of my three-day excursion in northern Saskatchewan," Ty said brightly. "In case you're just joining us, allow me to recap. The crew and I got dumped from our dogsled, lashed by a late-season blizzard, found an emergency shelter, only to have it burst into flames in the dead of night, and now we're trudging back along the sled trail, where we don't actually know which route to take to meet the safety crew. I have a confession to tender, as well—I ate half an orange that my camera crew packed for their lunch. So sue me. At least I won't get scurvy." He flashed his charming smile.

Ty went on for a while, riffing, explaining creosote fires and expounding on some of the features of the landscape, but Kate wasn't listening. She watched him in the viewfinder, trying to square the man she was recording with the one she'd made love to. He was good…. He *could* do this by himself. He could do this in his sleep, if he ever got any. He could certainly do this with someone else….

"Kate?" Ty on the tiny screen prompted.

"Sorry, what?"

"I'm all out of half-cocked nonsense to blather at you."

"Oh, right." She shut the camera off.

"That boring, eh? Well, the one thing you don't do for me is narration, so I guess that's to your credit."

"I don't feel like talking, Ty. I'm really tired."

"Okay." He looked up at the sky for a moment. "Do you feel like singing? You want to do 'Paradise by the Dashboard Light' with me? You can be Meat Loaf."

"No, Ty."

"Just trying to cheer you up," he said, catching her obvious irritation.

"I'm fine."

"You look sad." He cleared his throat. "I'm not used to you looking that way."

"Will you let me keep my job? All of it?"

"Not the filming bits."

"Then get used to me looking sad."

Ty turned her by the arm so they were facing and halted. "I don't mean to flog a dead horse, but I can't help but think you care more about this than…than anything."

"Exactly."

"Sorry, Kate, but that's not okay." He suddenly looked and sounded very impassioned. "I'm not worth sacrificing everything for. You can't do this, and get hurt or killed because of me."

"Ty—"

"And don't try and tell me it's your choice, like that's what this is about. This is about me having to live with it, if anything ever happened to you. This is self-preservation, trust me."

"How noble of you."

He shook his head, frustrated, but released her so they could continue the hike. "I never claimed to be some self-sacrificing saint."

"No, more like suicidal." She turned the thought over in her head and came up thoroughly annoyed. "You have a hell of a nerve, you know. Getting all protective of me, when I can't even get you to buckle your seat belt or look both ways before you cross the street. I've spent three seasons sitting by and respecting your, frankly idiotic, way of doing things. At first I thought, well, maybe it's good TV. Ty sets himself up for some calculated danger so he can show the audience how to get out of a jam, hey, good for the show. But that's not it, is it?"

"Kate—"

"Now I *nearly* get hurt in a perfectly accidental crash, and suddenly the risk is too great. That's so amazingly hypocritical I could just…I could scream at you. What is it with you? Why are like this? Is it some adrenaline addiction thing, or do you actually want to die young?"

"I don't want to die," he said quietly.

"Oh no? Well, act like it."

He kept his eyes on the ground ahead of him, pace steady, lips pursed in a tight line.

"Why then, Ty?"

"I just…" He sighed, clearly angry. "I just have to be sure that I'm supposed to still be here."

It was Kate's turn to sigh. "What do you mean, still be here?"

He glanced up and held her eyes for a second before turning back to the slushy trail. "Something happened, when I was little. This awful thing…"

"What?"

"Somebody died. It should have been me, but it wasn't."

She stopped in her tracks. "What do you mean? Who died?"

Ty stopped, too. "My little sister."

"You had a sister? You never told me."

"You never told me you had a fiancé," he countered.

"What happened to her?" Kate asked, dread gurgling in her middle. She stared at his face, his expression one she'd never seen before…sad and cold and grim. "Ty?"

Ty starting walking again. "I was seven and she was six, and we were playing on a dock at my uncle's place on the ocean. She dared me to jump off and I was scared, because it seemed really high up. She got fed up with me…she was always like that. Always busting everybody's balls, even that young. Anyway, she jumped first, and she got carried off by a riptide and drowned. Jesus. She was only six."

Kate bit her lip, studying his face. The iciness was gone now, leaving only sadness. "Ty…you couldn't have saved her. Not from a riptide. You'd both have probably drowned if you'd tried."

"No. But if I hadn't been scared in the first place…"

"Then you'd have died."

He nodded faintly, looking at the ground in front of him. "Anyway. That's why I won't do an episode on the open ocean—I can't stand knowing that huge empty space swallowed up my sister. And that's why I hate hearing my first name, because I had to listen to her calling out for me to help her, while I just stood there, frozen." He blinked for a moment, looking annoyed. "That's why my parents are how they are, because they blame themselves."

Kate couldn't think of anything to say.

"And I'm sorry," he added, "because I know how much you hate for people to be so bloody trite."

His steps got quicker and Kate had to work to keep up. She wasn't sure of how to address him so she focused on her feet, on the trail, on the information he'd shared. It wasn't trite; it just explained him. Everything. Perfectly. About how he'd ended up the way he was, so obsessed with acting brave, to make up for the shame he must have felt for so long. What he lost sleep over every night. Why the idea of Kate getting hurt would upset him so much.

She cleared her throat. "I'm sure that wasn't your fault, Ty."

"And I'm sure you don't know the first thing about it." He wouldn't meet her eyes. "Let's do some more filming."

When she hesitated he took the camera from her, swapping back the axe. She fell mute as he recorded some first-person footage, disturbed by the off-camera change in him. If there was one thing Ty was *not,* it was angry. He'd been in the middle of more fights than any man she'd ever met, but he was always jumping in, prying people apart. Ty didn't do angry. He barely did irritated. He only ever raised his voice in celebration. Kate had seen him accosted by snakes, by natural disasters, by lies and insults from the entertainment press, but he'd never batted an eye before the sled accident. She watched him addressing the mic, the picture of confidence and self-possession. She'd never noticed it before, but he was one hell of a good actor.

10

A GOOD HALF-HOUR FARTHER along the trail, the sky still looked unsuitable for shooting off flares or assembling a signal fire. Ty glanced to where Kate was keeping his trudging pace without complaint. It wasn't beyond the realm of possibility that they might reach the safety crew's camp before the sky cleared. That suited him just fine—he wouldn't mind maintaining his current rescue-free track record. They were safe now, which was the main thing. The temperature was hovering around freezing but the wind had calmed. Ty's toes had stopped prickling and gone numb a couple of miles back, but frostbite didn't seem to be a major threat.

"How are your feet?" he asked Kate, breaking a long silence.

She looked down at them. "Still tingly. I'm wiggling my toes."

"Good."

"We should be at the fork soon," she said, sounding nervous. "I mean, we'd have noticed if we hit it already."

"I hope the rescue crew's all right."

"Unless their cabin caught on fire, too, I'm sure they are. Toasty warm and well fed."

Ty let himself imagine such a thing for a moment.

Electric heat. A working kitchen. A modern bloody bathroom. *Food.*

Kate laughed, a small huff of breath. "Who knows, maybe they got laid, too."

Ty winced. What had happened between them went so far beyond *getting laid.* He had half a mind to—

"Hey, look." Kate pointed ahead to where the trail split in two, both routes looking for all intents and purposes identical.

He felt his whole body tense, that old paralysis, his violent allergic reaction to decision making. "And you don't remember which way the team would have gone?"

She shook her head. "I only got the map yesterday morning from Grenier. I was busy breaking up dogfights."

"Well, what do you reckon? Left or right?"

"It's your show."

"And you're the brains behind it." Ty didn't think he could stand being in charge of picking for the both of them. If he chose wrong and something else went awry he doubted he'd be able to stomach the guilt.

"Why don't we decide the Dom Tyler way?" Kate asked. "Do you have a coin?"

His chest loosened. "No…but we could flip your glove, maybe." Her gloves were black on the palm sides, striped on the backs.

She slipped one off. "You be left. I'll be right. You call it." She flung the glove up into the air.

"Stripes."

It landed black side up.

"I win," she said with a small smile, a little taste of how they used to be. How they'd been for two and a half years, until this stupid, ill-fated trip. "Right it is," Kate said, tugging her glove back on.

Ty felt a wash of sweet relief, not only from her warming

tone but also from having the universe put firmly back in charge. Accept all dares, let chance sort out the rest—the philosophy he lived by. Whenever possible, he let the flip of a coin or the toss of a dart make his decisions. Left or right, north or south, life or death… In the case of the latter, chance always chose life. Ty couldn't imagine why. That karma seemed so bent on knocking now, ready to collect on Ty's debt while Kate was here with him…well, that just stood to reason. After two-plus decades of gambling with fate, he should have caught on that his own life wasn't a big enough ante.

They started down their blameproof route of more unending white snow, and black forest. How odd that it'd probably be a balmy seventy-plus when they disembarked at LAX the next day, or whenever they managed to make it back to the "real world."

"Do you want some string cheese? Or nuts?" Kate had her calm blue eyes aimed at him, a ceasefire inherent in her tight smile.

"Nah. Let's let that orange be my one-and-only transgression."

"As you wish. Hold up a second."

Ty stood still while Kate dug a crinkling bag out of the pack strapped to his back. He propped the camera on his shoulder when she finished fussing and got her in focus.

"How are you enjoying the overnight, Kate Somersby?"

"The crappy motor lodges are looking like the Ritz, after last night," she told the lens, popping cashews in her mouth. "And I can't wait to brush my teeth and change my frigging underwear."

"Somersby…I never noticed before, but that's a pretty posh name you've got. For a girl who keeps insisting she's from the wrong side of the tracks."

Ty filmed her shrug. "The Somersbys of Dorchester, Massachusetts."

She cocked her eyebrow. "I changed my name, okay, Ty?"

"Oh yeah? What was it before?"

"Sullivan."

"Ah. But you've always been a Kate?"

She nodded.

"What's wrong with Kate Sullivan?"

"I don't know…it's just so…Boston. I wanted to get as far away from my roots as I could."

"Like a reinvention?"

"I guess."

"I'd like to meet the old Kate, Kate."

Another shrug. "Like I said, Ty, people don't change. You're looking at her right now, minus the trashy accent and the tacky lip liner."

"I'd like to hear your accent. You've heard mine."

"No way."

"How does it go? It's all 'cah pahking,' right?"

"Thet's roight, mate," she said, imitating Ty's Australian pronunciation.

"Ooh, not too shabby." Ty smiled at her for the first time in quite a while. He lowered the camera so she could see. "I missed you, Katie."

She looked away.

"And I still want to kiss you. Will you let me?"

KATE SHRUGGED, CONSIDERING Ty's request. She was wary of what another kiss would do to her, but she was also dead tired and didn't think Ty stood much chance of rousing anything in her aside from a bit of limp, apathetic receptivity. And secretly, underneath the exhaustion and irritation, she *did* want to kiss him. He'd shared something intensely personal with her earlier on this hike, and she wanted to underscore that intimacy, before it went away for good.

"Yeah, fine," she said.

Ty smiled deeper, fixing his eyes on hers. He dropped the pack from his shoulders and balanced the camera on it. "Put the axe down? It's a bit unnerving."

Kate complied, smirking to herself but feeling suddenly nervous. "I'm going to taste like cashews."

"I'll have to own up to that to the viewers, I suppose," Ty said as he closed in, voice already turning hushed from The Shift. He pulled his gloves off and shoved them into his pocket. He ran his hands up her arms, her shoulders, her scarf-clad neck, just as he had so many times before. Their eyes flickered together, faces close. She could feel his energy, her body beginning to vibrate at that familiar frequency.

Ty's eyes closed as he brought his mouth to hers, grazing skin against skin, cautious. Kate's lips were tender from everything that had gone on in the past eighteen hours. Their noses touched as his fingertips alighted on her jaw. Parting her lips to welcome his, she felt all the exhaustion and angst and doubt leaving her, melting away, until all that was left was the two of them and their point of contact. Ty deepened the kiss, his hot tongue sliding against hers, sending the blush from her cheeks flashing down her body, to her breasts and belly, and then down between her legs. Damn, that boy could kiss. She angled her head to invite his explorations. She moved her hands to his jacket, unzipping it and wrapping her arms around him inside. She felt his arousal before long, his cock pressing against her navel, insistent. Scenes from the previous night flashed through her mind—Ty's body, big and strong and demanding, his face as he approached climax, those eyes burning into hers.

They kissed for a minute, maybe ten, maybe an hour.

When Ty pulled away, Kate could have sworn the previously monochrome woods were on fire, everything impossibly bright and saturated in the wake of their embrace.

"We should keep moving," Ty said, voice husky. He licked his flushed lips, his eyes still locked on hers.

"I suppose so." Kate reluctantly released him.

His gaze zigzagged over her face and there was something wild in his expression. Something beyond The Shift, even. She caught him glancing over her shoulder as he put his hands on her upper arms, walking her clumsily backward until her back pressed against a tree trunk, just like the day before.

"Ty," she murmured, unsure herself if it was protest or encouragement.

He crossed his mouth over hers again, hungry. Ravenous. Small, desperate noises drifted from his throat, thrilling Kate deep inside. The conflict disappeared along with the vulnerability, and all that was left was the two of them. Two people who'd sheltered together under strange and exotic circumstances, as well as mundane ones. Sequestered in complete geographic isolation, and also in the midst of bustling industry parties, all the time each wanting this but unwilling to ask for it. Never in her life had Kate craved a man the way she had Ty, and never in her dreams had she imagined how utterly satisfying the reality of him would be. She might be losing this when they got back to the city, but she wouldn't let *this* moment pass her by. A hundred blizzards couldn't dampen the fire between them.

Kate sensed Ty's self-control dissolving as his lips crossed her cheek to her ear, then her jaw. Impatient hands tugged down the zipper of her coat. His touch roamed over her, surveying her with rough caresses as she cradled his head in her gloved hands. His mouth teased the skin uncovered by her scarf. The breath caught in her lungs as his hands found the waistband of her hiking pants, and she felt her body's demand breaching the dam that held her back, liquid heat collecting between her thighs.

She uttered his name, the tiny syllable nearly choking her.

"God, Kate." She felt his lips moving as he spoke, just as his fingers slipped inside her panties, the coldness of his skin making her own heat seem that much more fiery by comparison. "Spread your legs for me," he whispered, and she widened her stance to give him the access he demanded.

His slippery touch felt like one she'd known for years, belonging to a lover more dear and familiar than any she'd ever come close to actually having. He rubbed her clit with the pads of two fingers. He hooked them, dipping inside her with a harsh moan and reminding her of another part of him…reminding her of something she ached for a thousand times more desperately than she'd craved food or warmth just minutes earlier. Behind his head her hands stripped off their gloves and dropped them to the ground.

As her nails scraped his scalp, Ty intensified his touch. Kate wanted more. She flirted briefly with the hard contours hidden behind his sweater. Her hands went in search of his belt. The sound of that very buckle hitting the ground who-knew-how-many times during their immodest professional relationship had never failed to thrill her. Now, fumbling then feeling it release in her own hands, she whimpered from the overwhelming longing it triggered. Her fingers quaked as she unbuttoned his jeans. As the zipper slid down over the stiff ridge of his arousal, Ty panted at her throat, his strong body pinning her to the tree by her shoulder. Any discomfort she felt only fueled the pleasure.

"Yes," he whispered, thrusting his hips against her palm

as she wrapped her fingers around his cock, sheathed in cotton.

She whispered against his ear. "You keep me up nights, Ty."

He seemed to lose the ability to form words, reduced to primitive sounds—the same ones she'd heard him make two years earlier, ones that had haunted her memory when they were the spoils of some other woman's victory. But now these sounds were hers. All this animal need was hers to satisfy.

"Say my name, Ty," she breathed.

"Katie." His free hand grew demanding, forcing its way between them to push his underwear down and release his hard, bare cock into her eager hand. His fingers, stoking the fire in her core, trembled faintly.

"Did you fantasize about this?" Kate asked, lips against his temple, luxuriating in this tall, powerful body bent close to dominate hers.

"All the bloody time."

Kate tortured him with long, slow pulls. Her own breath became shallow as his fingers coaxed her closer to the edge. She remembered everything that had gone on just a few hours before in the dancing, warming light of the woodstove. Her fingers gripped him tighter, her touch quickening as she handled him roughly, rising to the level of intensity she herself craved—rising to the level of the frantic energy his hips had delivered when they'd made love, giving all that pleasure to her.

"You felt so amazing inside me, Ty. I'm thinking about it now."

He groaned and she felt the damp skin of his forehead on her temple, beading with sweat even in the bitter cold. A third finger entered her, exciting her, driving her toward the free fall.

"Don't stop, Ty."

"Am I going to make you come?" he whispered. His body tightened perceptibly against hers.

"Just don't stop." Her hips were greedy now, riding his fingers, reliving her memories.

"Come on, Katie." He put his own free hand over the fist she had wrapped around him, squeezing it tight, his hips thrusting in time. His forehead pressed against hers. His eyes narrowed with feverish excitement, their blue-green heat burning into her own.

A tremor of pure pleasure jarred Kate's entire body in erratic waves, centered against Ty's relentless touch, radiating out and erupting from her lungs in a feral, otherworldly groan. His touch slowed as her body clenched him tight, but he didn't leave her.

"God, Ty." She gulped for air, trying to regain the use of her limbs. A strong, masterful hand kept her stroking him until she was in control once more.

"I'm so close," he moaned, and his fingers inside her trembled, reigniting her excitement.

"Come on, Ty. Come for me."

Her eyes darted from the handsome features of his disbelieving face down between their bodies, at the dark mauve of the head of his cock, the size of him, the thickness, at her own hand as it pleasured him. He lost himself. He slid her palm up to cup his head, squeezing it tight until she felt him come—the scalding, wet heat of his release in her hand—and just as he did she was taken by an aftershock, left bucking a second time against his fingers.

"Oh, Kate." He craned his head back as his body stilled. His hands wrapped around her inside her coat, pinning them together. The embrace went on until both their heartbeats slowed again and the heat began to wane. Ty stepped back a pace and drew the zipper up the front of her coat.

In silence they tidied their clothes, donned their gloves and gathered up the supplies. All at once Kate remembered how cold it was. Ty zipped his own jacket back up and it felt like a door being shut in her face. Their last encounter as lovers. The closing of a brief but overwhelmingly complex chapter. It was almost a relief.

They walked without speaking for a half mile or more, until Ty shattered the peace, giving a voice to Kate's sad thoughts.

"You didn't answer my question, before."

"Which question?"

"When we get back to L.A.," he began, cautious, "is it still going to be like this?"

"Like what?"

"You know. You and me…"

"Lovers?" she prompted.

"Mmm."

Kate made a reckless decision, the choice turning her stomach but seeming the only thing to say. "No, Ty. This was just physical, wasn't it?"

"Maybe."

"It was. It's okay. And anyway, I know your schedule. Better than you do. Literally. You'll be too busy to see me. I'll be busy, too, working for someone else, if I can't change your mind. So no. You and me, in the woods—this is all we get."

"I see." He was impossible to read.

"Don't worry, Ty. Like I said, it was the hottest sex of my life."

"Well. Glad to know it meant something to you."

She nodded absently.

"And that's all it was to you, then? Satisfying a curiosity?"

"So what if it was?"

Ty frowned. "Jesus, Kate…"

"What?" she cut in.

"I wish, just once, you'd let me see you with your bloody armor off."

"Like how?" she demanded.

"Just…be vulnerable in front of me. Let me think that there's some depth to us.…" His eyes roamed her face, pleading. "I want so badly to think that this is more than just professional. And now sexual. You're my best friend, you know. I trust you more than anybody else in the whole world. Nobody's as much fun as you, or knows me as well as you do. It kills me that you don't feel the same way. Just tell me there's something special here, because I'm starting to think I imagined it all."

Kate started. It was exactly how she'd felt that morning. It stirred her. And, oddly, it calmed her.

"I *do* think you're my best friend. I *know* you are," she amended. "And it's not that I don't trust you…I dunno. I'm just careful."

Ty sighed, sounding so defeated it broke her heart.

"What do I mean to you, Katie? Honestly?"

The question ripped through her, left her feeling flayed wide-open, exposed. She thought about it, and the word *everything* was all that came to mind, though it was also far too much to say out loud. Still, all the emotion she'd been suppressing was building, aching to come out before it consumed her. Ty was being straight with her and she owed him a taste of that in return.

She opened her mouth, hesitated, closed it, then opened it again. "Do you…?" Her throat tightened.

"Do I what, Kate?"

"Do you remember, a couple years ago, after we wrapped the first season…?"

"Mmm?"

She exhaled a loaded breath, concentrated on her trudging feet. "There was a party. You got tickets from someone at the network to this cocktail party at a trendy bar, after a premiere of some movie or other. We went together because whoever you were dating was out of town and you didn't want to miss out on free shrimp."

Ty smiled. "I remember."

"We danced, that night. I was about half-drunk and we slow danced to an old soul song, and it was like prom night for me, for a few minutes." Her body warmed at the memory. "You were dressed up. You had on a white dress shirt, one I'd bought for you for some other event. You took your tie off about ten minutes into the party and made me put it in my purse because you said it was strangling you. And the top couple buttons of your shirt were undone and your sleeves were rolled up, and you'd shaved. I had heels on but my chin still only came up to your collar, and I rested it there and you smelled…" She had to close her eyes and take another steadying breath from the mere memory of it, even now.

"You smelled so amazing. It was just your cologne or aftershave, but you smelled like…I don't know. Like the 1950s. Like Scotch and cedar or something else. Like a film star. You were the best-looking man in the whole bar. In the whole world, and I was dancing with you. It was as if I was in a movie. And you were so warm and you were holding one of my hands and when the song ended I had to excuse myself to go to the bathroom because I thought I was going to cry."

Ty didn't reply, his eyes looking cautious as they darted over her face.

"And that was the best and worst night of my entire life," Kate concluded. She shuddered faintly, surprised that sharing this hadn't hurt the way she'd assumed it would. She tugged on her earlobe, waiting for Ty to make fun of her, but feeling prepared to handle it.

He cleared his throat and stared off beyond her shoulder, thoughtful. "It was 'Cruisin',' by Smokey Robinson."

She blinked. "Pardon?"

"That was the song that was playing. I bought the album the next day. You were wearing a dress the color of…I dunno. Something red, but *redder*. With little sparkly things near the neck. Your hair was down. It looked so shiny under the lights that I thought my drink must have been spiked."

She blushed and stared down at the slushy ground. "I don't remember what I was wearing."

"I do. And you smelled like lilies. Your hands and the skin between your shoulder blades was insanely soft, and when I got home that night I thought about taking that dress off of you and making love to you in my bed. I thought about burying my face in your hair and burying myself deep inside your body and feeling you come against me. And afterward I felt like a complete bastard and I knew I had to break up with Angie when she got back to the city."

Kate's heart pounded, as hard as it had when she'd been in the cab with him on the way back to their apartments that night, drunk on the evening and the champagne and wondering with shameful excitement if he might try to come up to her place. He hadn't. He'd just said good-night and thanked her for being his last-minute date and said he'd see her the next day for work.

"You've ruined every relationship I've tried to have since we met, Katie."

"I didn't mean to."

"No, I know. But you did. And you'll keep ruining them. I won't even bother trying anymore, actually. There's no point. I won't be able to leave the house for a night, anyway, in case it might be the night you decide you're finally going to come over and be with me again."

She swallowed, afraid of everything he was saying. "Don't."

"I can't be without you, Katie. I'm so lost when you're not around."

"You'll find another PA," she said.

"That's not what I mean and you know it."

She paused. "It won't work, Ty. We only work now because we're both in charge."

His eyebrow rose. "And what does that mean?"

"It means the way things are now, we both get to be in control. You're my boss. But I tell you what to do. You're going to take away my power and I won't be able to be this way with you."

"I've never thought about us that way."

"Well, I have. It's the reason we work. *Worked.* You only get me if you let me keep this job," she said, laying her cards on the table.

"Oh." She expected a further challenge, but he didn't offer one.

"So I guess it's an ultimatum."

"I can't chance losing you again," he said.

"*You* can't leave something to chance? That's a riot, Ty." The bitterness in her voice shifted the atmosphere between them like a spike in the air pressure.

His eyes narrowed. "Maybe some things are worth trying to protect. You know, I think a lot of people would say we've both got pretty buggered-up priorities, but maybe I'm capable of changing mine."

"You know how I feel about change," she said.

He frowned outright. "So what do you want, Kate? You want to end up with some man who lets you boss him around and run his life? Is that what you'll settle for because being the one wearing the pants is so bloody important to you?"

"It's your fault I have to settle in the first place."

"What does that mean?"

She warmed to the debate. "We could have been everything together. Partners, lovers, friends. Everything. This could've been perfection. You and me, traveling the world, having great sex and a fantastically fun time together, getting paid to do it all. And we still could, if you'd just let me keep my job. Let go of your ridiculous fear about my safety and we can still have an amazing couple of years together before the show wraps."

Ty shook his head. "I don't want you on terms, Kate. I need to believe you care more about being with me than having these…power dynamics."

"Yeah, well, this is me. This is how I am. And I won't change for you or for anybody. I can't change. Trust me, I've tried. I thought I'd buried the old me, left her behind in Massachusetts when I moved to L.A. But I get it now—I'm still her. Different clothes and résumé, but here I am, still following some man around like a masochistic puppy. It's all pointless. People don't change."

"So you keep reminding me."

"Just like you can't help but try to prove to everybody how brave you are, to make up for what happened when you were a kid."

Ty's posture hitched, as if he'd bumped into an invisible obstacle. "That's what you think I'm about? That I'm always trying to prove something? You meant that?"

"That's what everyone thinks, Ty. And it's true."

"You don't know me at all," he said, quiet and stony.

"Then why? Why, if you don't have some need to show everybody what huge frigging balls you have now; to make up for what happened?"

He stopped walking. "I do it because I need to know that I'm not supposed to be dead yet."

Kate stopped, too, and furrowed her brow. "What does that even mean?"

"It means I should've been the one who died that day, instead of my sister. And yeah, if I'd been brave enough to take her dare, she'd probably still be around, not me. So every chance I get, I throw myself in front of the bus, because I don't know if I'm even supposed to be here. And I *keep. Bloody. Not. Dying.*"

Kate stared at him, confused.

Ty went on. "I should have died about a thousand times now. From rubbish I got up to as a kid, and climbing accidents or rushing into other people's fights, or any other mad thing I've done. I'll do anything, as long as nobody else has to depend on me. And now you—you depend on me. And on this trip I let you down for the first time. I've been tempting fate, but now it's after you. And that's not okay."

"That's ridiculous," Kate said. "The universe isn't out to get me, and you're not, I dunno…immune to dying. You're wrong, Ty. I mean, if you really believe this is some kind of destiny bull or whatever—and don't take this the wrong way—why don't you just kill yourself?"

"It doesn't work that way."

"What doesn't work what way?" she asked, exasperated.

"I value my life. But I have to keep testing it. I need to know that it's okay that I'm still here."

"Well fine, Ty. You *are* supposed to be here. Obviously. The universe wants you alive, so deal with it. Have a happy, safe life and stop torturing yourself."

Ty's eyes scanned the woods, restless. "I really thought you knew me, Katie."

"Like I said, I *know* you. I just don't understand you. Not the you that you don't show everybody. But I…I like you when you're a mess. When you come knocking on my door and you can't sleep. I wanted to think that I was the only person who got to see that." She ran her palm over her heart, trying to ease the fear tightening her chest. "I wanted to think you needed me. Just me. Nobody else."

He met her eyes. "You don't think I do?"

Her foot hit a rock hidden under the snow and she tripped, the cold spray of slush worsening her already lousy mood. "I don't feel like I know anything anymore," she said. "But if you'd see my side of things, at least one of us would get our way, Ty. And our lives could just go on the way they have been."

"Haven't you ever messed up, Kate? Hasn't anything terrible ever happened because of something you did, or something you didn't do? Haven't you ever lost anyone close to you and had to plead with the universe to make sense of it?"

She stopped walking and whipped around to face him. "I'm about to lose someone, yes. And I don't plead for things, but if I did I'd be on my knees, begging you to see what a huge mistake you're making."

"Haven't you lost someone, though? Anybody who meant something to you? When your dad left? When your fiancé ditched you? Didn't you wonder what you could have done to prevent it?"

"No, Ty, I didn't. My dad was never really there, even when he was. I lived with my mom for almost twenty years and she wasn't there, either." Kate locked her arms around her middle, feeling naked. She watched Ty's throat move as he swallowed.

"Was she abusive, or…?"

"She wasn't mean.… She just wasn't…there. She was like

a ghost or something. She'd already hemorrhaged whatever love she had in her for eight ungrateful kids and a deadbeat disappointment of a husband. There wasn't anything left by the time I showed up. I literally went weeks without her even making eye contact with me," Kate said, hating the unsteady sound of her own voice. "But that wasn't my fault—it's just the crappy hand I drew."

"But it made you how you are," he said. "All self-sufficient and independent."

Kate gave a cold laugh. "Made me into a smothering, clingy psycho in high school, more like. I befriended and dated anybody who gave me any kind of attention, and all that taught me was that pathetic, needy girls scare the living crap out of people. I don't miss anyone I've left behind, or who's left me." *And if you leave me,* she thought, *it'll be the first time I'll have to say goodbye to someone who matters. But don't expect me to grovel.* "So there you go. There's me in a sad little nutshell. Boo hoo."

Ty didn't respond, just held her gaze for a few seconds before he started walking again, taking the lead.

Kate pushed a long sigh through her nose and felt some relief in the wake of the rant, her anger dissipating in tiny measures along with the vapor of her breath. There were other things she'd have been tempted to tell Ty if he hadn't backed her into a corner. She'd have wanted to tell him that the fun they used to have on the road was like compensation for all the irresponsible joy she'd missed out on as a child. That those nights he came to her room to be soothed and distracted were the first and only times she'd ever felt needed or valued or wanted in her entire life. With a shake of her head she dismissed the impulse to tell him these things. It was bad enough that she'd let him in as deep as she had.

"I'm not leaving you, Kate," he murmured. "I just want

to guarantee nothing bad will happen to you. I'm doing this because I can't stand the thought of you leaving *me*. Permanently."

"You're doing it because you're picking this ridiculous survivor's guilt bullshit over what we could have."

She watched Ty's jaw flex as he thought. "And you're picking your need to bloody control everything."

Kate sighed silently to herself. "Yeah, I am."

"I guess I see where we stand, then—" Ty fell silent as a sound in the distance became audible to them, then grew louder.

Motors.

11

TY STRAINED FOR CONFIRMATION, the sound too wonderful to be real.

"Snowmobiles," Kate said, eyes widening. "The safety crew!"

"Or somebody, anyhow. Get out of the middle of the trail." They stood a few feet from the woods and waited, poised to hail their rescuers as the hum of motors grew louder, perhaps a half mile away. Ty held his breath, listening to the beautiful sound of their salvation approaching.

Then as quickly as it had come, the noise faded.

He stepped forward, looking all around. "Uh-oh."

The snowmobiles were on some other, parallel trail—the other side of the fork, now a two-hour walk back in the direction they'd come from or a who-knew-how-long trek through the dense woods.

"Oh, no! Hey! Hey! Help!" Kate screamed in the direction of the dying noise, waving her arms and the axe, but they'd never be able to hear her over the din of the motors.

"Bollocks," Ty groaned.

"Oh, *God*." Slumping against a nearby tree, Kate succumbed to defeat. Wallowed in it, by the look of her face.

Ty could relate. Another two hours of this. And then what? No helicopters would be able to look for them in this fog, and it could easily take a couple of hours for the rescue team to spot a signal fire or come upon them on the trail again. Well, at least they knew which route was correct.

"Sorry, Kate."

She sighed, sounding too exhausted now to stay angry with him. "It's okay…we'll get home. I'm just so frigging tired."

He nodded, accepting her unarticulated truce.

"Let's just cut through the woods, toward the other trail," she said. "I can't walk back all that way. I'll go crazy."

"We can try," Ty said. "But we might miss them if they come up this branch."

"Let's split up, then. One of us can cut through to the other trail, and whoever grabs the rescue guys first can take them to where the other is."

"No way. You have any idea how many times I've preached on camera how stupid it is to split up in the wilderness? And out here?" He waved an arm around the cold and homogenous landscape, a perfect recipe for getting lost and disoriented.

"I'm trained, Ty, same as you. We've got compasses— one in the pack and one on my watch. Seriously. We'll stay within shouting distance. But if the snowmobiles come by again and we miss them… Forget my sanity, okay? Just save my toes. We're so close."

He scanned the woods, uneasy. "Shouting distance?"

"Every minute, you shout, I'll shout back. That's got to be a half mile, maybe more. Maybe close enough for whoever's cutting through to make a run for the other trail if the rescue team comes back. Flag them down."

"I don't like it."

"Please, Ty?"

The look on her face did him in. He'd never seen her so helpless before, so openly pleading.

"Fine. But only on those conditions."

"That's fine." Kate took her glove off again. "Stripes, I'll stay on this trail. Black, I'll cut through the woods."

Ty nodded and she tossed the glove into the air. Once again it landed black-side-up.

"What supplies do you want?" she asked as she pulled it back on.

"I'm fine with just the compass. You keep the pack."

"Okay…" Kate trailed off, shifty eyes darting through the woods. "I'm leaving you the camera, though."

Ty smiled grimly. "Of course you are."

"Can—"

"Lots of footage, yes, no worries." Ty rolled his eyes, dropped Kate's frame pack off his shoulders, grabbed the compass clipped to the front pocket. She adjusted the straps and shrugged it on. They exchanged an awkward glance, neither able to look the other fully in the eye.

"Well," she finally said. "I guess this is where we go our separate ways."

Ty nodded, hating her word choice, hating the fact that she chose it in lieu of a good old honest kick to his balls. "I'll see you soon," he said. "Lakers tickets say I find the rescue crew first."

Kate smiled, just a tiny sliver of how they were supposed to be, but it warmed Ty nonetheless. "You're on."

She offered him a tight, melancholy smile and a wave of her gloved hand, then turned away, walked directly into the woods and left him behind.

As much as Kate wanted to blindly propel herself away from Ty, she mustered the good sense not to waste all her years of on-the-job training. She rolled up her sleeve and checked the compass on her watch, noting that she was heading northwest so she could check in five minutes that she was still making a straight line. It was tough, surrounded by all these uniform, scraggly black trees and white snow. Easy to get turned around.

In the distance, she heard Ty's shout, loud and clear. "Marco!"

She rolled her eyes and bellowed right back. "Polo!"

Kate had never been in the wilderness without Ty by her side, and it was unnerving. Unnerving but liberating. She'd be without him from now on, period, but she'd live. Her eyes jumped between the trees, on the lookout for any of the animals she'd seen listed in all the research she'd helped conduct on the region. None scared her too badly.... The worst were wolves and bobcats, but given the sled trail's relative noisiness and activity, she was willing to bet the animals stuck to the real woods. And even there, when Ty had been desperately looking for any creature at all to snare for his meals the first two days in the bush, they'd spotted next to nothing. A goose, those eggs, the occasional emaciated rodent.

"Marco!" Fainter, now, but still clear.

"Polo!"

Kate trudged onward, went into the meditation she'd routinely called on to escape the drudgery of the wilderness. She fantasized about her apartment, her favorite restaurants, the movie release dates she'd marked on her calendar. The bubble of happy anticipation grew, then deflated. All those places were better with Ty.

Whatever. She didn't *need* him. She wouldn't die without him, or this job. The shock was fading, morphing into mourning, but that too would pass. If life had taught Kate anything, it was that she couldn't make someone the center of her world. Yet here she'd done it again—moved to L.A. to escape her old, clingy self and woken up a helpless satellite caught in Ty's gravity. She'd fallen in love with him, like the incurable idiot she was.

"Marco!"

"Polo!"

At least she hadn't told him so. That was an improvement. Kate still fell hard, but she'd learned to save face.

Aside from their intermittent shouts, the woods were silent and lonely. She checked the compass and adjusted her course a little. Her feet ached, alternately cold and eerily warm, stiff and tingly. She missed music, missed the drone of her TV as she puttered in her home during the show's off-season. She wondered if maybe she'd get a cat now that she'd be around more. Or at the very least some houseplants…

Three things happened at once. A dull, mechanical snap sounded, shocking pain engulfed Kate's ankle and her own scream pierced the silence. She doubled over, grabbing her leg and falling on to her side. A metal trap was snapped tight around her foot, two hinged jaws biting into her skin. She stared at the black steel, her mind fighting her body's animal panic. She gulped deep breaths, willed herself calm.

"It's not broken," she told herself, half believing it. Her ankle was screaming with pain, but she prayed it hadn't fractured. This wasn't a bear trap—the jaws were smaller and unserrated, designed for big cats or maybe wolves. Kate suffered through the pain of relocating her butt, scooting forward to pull at the trap. Nothing—she couldn't budge the spring-loaded jaws.

"Ty!" She screamed it as loud as she could, prayed it might cover the distance now separating them. She tried prying at the trap again. No use. She swore a blue streak, shouted Ty's name until her throat burned. She couldn't make out a reply. Her head was consumed by a rushing noise, like radio static filling her up and dulling her awareness. She blinked and tiny white blobs danced in front of her eyes. She fumbled through her pack, tried using the handle of her folded utility knife to lever the jaws apart. It budged millimeters, if that.

"Crap. Crap crap crap." Kate tugged at her bad ear as a dark, crippling helplessness engulfed her. She felt alone not just in the woods but in the world—abandoned, forgotten. The pain in her leg intensified, metal clamping bone, the damage to her skin hidden behind her thick hiking pants and wool socks. Thank goodness for those. But something was off, beyond the pain…darkness was seeping into her head, dulling her thoughts. Her lungs raced for breath against her will, her heart beating wildly, so fast it terrified her. She felt an invisible hand closing on her throat. Kate fought the feeling, clawed through the pack and got the gun out, two flares still left in it. The last thing she was aware of before the shock won out was the bang as she squeezed the trigger, the spark as it shot up through the treetops.

"KATE? KATIE?"

Ty had been running full tilt through the trees, but now he slowed. Kate had stopped yelling and he didn't know where he was supposed to be heading. There were no tracks to help him, as he was coming from a totally different angle than she'd been traveling. He squinted for her bright green coat through the woods, but nothing.

Pop. Ty's head snapped up at the crackling of a flare and he could just make out the glittering of red light against the cloudy sky.

"Kate?" he shouted. Still nothing, but he ran once again, dodging trees, dodging mental images of Kate clinging to the broken ice in some frigid, snow-hidden pond, dropping below the surface. God, how could he have let her go like that? The one time he knew which decision to make and he let her talk him out of it. Idiot.

Ty jogged until his lungs burned, his throat dry from the icy air and his intermittent shouts. Then, there it was—a sliver of leaf-green nylon in the distance.

"Kate!" Ty sprinted the last hundred slippery, slushy yards, his heart hammering as he found her lying on her side, pack open and supplies scattered beside her. He slid to a halt and sank to his knees, touching her face and hair, confused. Her eyes were open and her breaths raced in violent bursts, endless puffs of fog between her lips.

"Kate? Can you hear me? What's wrong?"

No sign of acknowledgment. Ty didn't need one. He needed only to get her to safety. Just as he was about to hoist her into his arms, he saw the black chain stretched from her foot across the snow.

"Oh, God." He scrambled to inspect it, relieved there was no blood. But she was in some kind of shock; she had to be. That meant she'd suffered horrible pain, and that could easily mean a broken bone. Ty didn't know a ton about traps, but enough to wonder if this one was illegal, given the area and the time of year. Thankfully he knew how to open it. He gently angled Kate's knee so her foot was flat on the ground and got himself to standing. Each side of the trap had a spring mechanism that jutted out. Ty pinned one to the ground with his foot and did the same to the other to release the tension. He eased the jaws apart and gingerly lifted Kate's foot out. The metal slapped shut again as he stepped away and stooped to haul Kate into his arms.

She was a small woman but the shock racking her body made her a pile of twitchy dead weight. No matter—Ty would carry her all the way to L.A. if he had to. He left the pack, axe and camera on the ground, aimed himself in the direction Kate had been heading, and just walked.

As he walked, Ty felt strange—more lucid and focused than he could ever remember being in his entire life. The black trees against the gray sky and the white snow were cast in such sharp relief that it felt surreal, as though he were traveling through a charcoal drawing. He could feel his heart beating, feel each ounce of blood humming through his veins. He'd been without food and rest for nearly four days, but somehow, with Kate's quaking body draped over his arms, he suspected he could run a marathon.

"Ty." She mouthed the word more than actually uttering it, eyes unfocused.

"Can you understand me? Can you hear me?"

No answer. Her breaths were raspy and rapid, terrifying.

"Hang in there, Katie. I'm going to get you home real soon," he promised. "We're going to get you warm, and fix your ankle. And if you even think about asking about the camera I'll throttle you."

He glanced down, saw Kate had succumbed to her hyperventilation and passed out. Her exhalations had slowed, her eyes closed. Ty swallowed and prayed that might be an improvement.

"If you promise you'll be okay," he said to Kate's inattentive face, "I'll give you anything you want. I'll even give you your stupid filming back, maybe. We'll do a whole season of open ocean scenarios. In the tropics. At Cannes. With celebrities. I'll wear a tux. Anything you want." He continued on this rant for a long time, bargaining with her using any and every currency he could think of. It struck him after a while that he wasn't bargaining with the universe for a change. There was a different source of meaning to his life now.

"And I'll even do that bloody *Esquire* interview and let them gel my hair—" His rambling cut off after about twenty minutes as the most glorious sight in the world met his eyes—the bright orange paint of the rescue team's parked snowmobiles in the distance. A few yards beyond stood the cabin where the team had set up.

"Hey!" Ty bellowed. He shouted it again and again, his lungs burning. He staggered onward, step by aching step, until the door opened.

THE FIRST THING KATE noticed as she regained consciousness was the sound of her own voice. She heard herself moaning before she felt it, and long before she could begin to control it. Behind the pitiful groans she heard Ty on her right.

"Katie?"

Then a woman's voice, difficult to make out on her left side. "Kate? Can you swallow?" The brim of a mug was pressed to her lips and the liquid that slid down her throat felt as if it must be boiling hot. She felt herself cough, heard Ty say, "Good girl."

They were inside and there was heat—steady heat, not fire. Electric lights. The woman holding the mug withdrew and Ty scooted his chair closer to touch Kate's hand, running his fingertips over her knuckles. His eyes looked darker, not lit by the sun for a change. They looked like the sea. She struggled to form words, her muscles uncooperative. The room seemed bright, like an overexposed photo and she felt trapped in her own body and unable to help herself—an old and very unwelcome sensation. Her first of many hurtful memories from her childhood, more than twenty years past but still more vivid than things she'd experienced even a month ago.

Ty sat patiently at her side, carrying on a rambling one-sided conversation for her entertainment, or possibly his own. Kate's bad ear ached, as badly as when she'd been four and had the infection that left her half-deaf. Her throat went tight, the muscles there remembering the hours she'd screamed and screamed from the pain, for nearly two days until her mother had finally had to accept that it was no mere tantrum. By then it'd been too late. By then she'd been doomed to a lifelong reminder of how inconsequential and inconvenient she was. Afterward, no apologies. No soothing or coddling. Just angry words about bills and insurance.

But this was so different. This time Ty was with her. Kate couldn't help it when she started to cry, and she hoped it would just look like a symptom of whatever had landed her here on her back. Ty's fingers wiped the tears from her face and more streamed out to replace them.

"Well, your tear ducts work," he said absently, thumbs running over her cheeks.

Kate wanted her muscles to comply so she could throw her arms around him and sob her appreciation into his shoulder. She felt herself smile weakly.

"There's an improvement." Ty offered her a smile in return.

She felt herself getting control again, her muscles obeying her brain's commands.

"Ty."

He smiled. "Can you hear me all right?"

"Yeah."

"Good. Can you see me?" He leaned in close and grinned at her.

"Yeah. Just fine."

His hands, warm and dry, cupped her face, thumbs stroking the feverish skin of her cheeks.

The image of the snow and black metal flashed across her mind, Ty's red coat, the treetops streaming by above her. "You saved me."

"Yeah. I guess I did."

"What happened?" she asked. "There was a trap."

"Yeah. Your ankle's okay—badly bruised, but not broken. And you hyperventilated. The medic thinks you went into shock from the pain."

From more than the physical pain, she thought. From a lifetime of emotional weight she'd been dragging around behind her, trying to ignore. She'd tamped it all down for years, that awful, helpless sensation, only to have it rush back the second that trap snapped around her ankle. Except this time, someone had cared. She stared into his eyes. "Are you angry at me? For making us split up?"

"No, Kate. I've never been happier in my entire life."

"Oh, good."

"But if you ever put me through anything like that again, I *will* murder you," he amended.

"Understood. I guess I like, *literally* don't have a leg to stand on now, trying to convince you this job isn't dangerous to my health."

Ty shook his head, not looking as if he wanted to pursue this conversation. Kate decided she didn't, either. She'd come out here and lost her job, but she'd found a lover, for as long as that might last. Right now she felt ready to surrender for a change, to take things as they came. She didn't want to hang on for dear life anymore, so scared of losing her grip that she couldn't enjoy anything. She wanted to let go, to float, the way she'd floated as Ty had carried her barely conscious body through the wilderness.

Then she thought of something else he might well wring her neck over. Her mouth opened and closed with uncertainty as she debated whether or not to ask about it.

Ty smirked grimly at her expression and read her mind. "Don't you even dare ask me about the bloody camera, you freak."

SEVERAL HOURS LATER KATE was up and moving with
the medic's permission, ankle puffy and sore but seeming
otherwise in good working order. While Kate had been
recuperating, two members of the crew had followed Ty's
tracks into the woods and recovered their abandoned equipment. Ty strapped the last of their stuff to the back of the
snowmobile and scanned the sky—still overcast but white
now, not gray. He ignored a rumble from his stomach, too
close to the finish line to give in and accept food from the
rescue crew. Anyhow, he'd break the fast properly, with a
steak and a beer, not a bag of crisps and a can of cola.

Soon enough they were back on the trail, Ty driving and
Kate huddled behind him, the rescue crew trailing a few
yards back. They zipped effortlessly over the snowy trails
he and Kate had been trudging along just hours before,
making the ordeal seem like a ridiculous dream.

The drone of the motor lulled his brain and he felt at
peace with the world. Accepting and calm. He couldn't quite
understand it. Ty's worst fear had just come to pass—Kate
had gotten hurt on his account. Times three. Sled accident,
creosote fire, trap… That last one was the worst. It had
been nearly twenty-five years since he'd stood by as another
person he loved made an impulsive decision, did what Ty
knew in his gut was wrong and made him watch as she
paid for it. And he'd let Kate go. He hadn't listened to his
gut, but goddamn, he'd *known* what to do—and it was the
right thing. He'd messed up again, he'd backed down. But
this time, when the consequences came, Ty hadn't frozen.
He'd come through for Kate, and there was no chance he'd
ever ignore his intuition again.

He knew now what had to be done about the show, and
Kate's job. He knew how to take his best stab at fixing
everything, and there was no chance he'd relent until he
got his way. No flip of the coin, no darts. He'd go after it

the patented Kate Somersby rabid-junkyard-dog way, the network be damned.

After an hour or so the trail opened onto a stretch of snow-covered prairie, and Ty spotted their salvation. Kate saw it, too—she squeezed his middle as Grenier's Sled Supply appeared on the horizon.

Jim Grenier must have been tipped off by the motors, because he was already walking down to meet them as they pulled off the trail.

"So, we didn't lose you, after all," he said, smiling at the pair of them as they dismounted and found their land legs.

"Nope," Ty said. "All your dogs made it back okay then?"

"They always do. I'm sure that camera you mounted on the sled's got a story to tell."

Kate went inside with Grenier to collect the items the dogs had brought back while Ty loaded the rental truck.

"It's going to feel weird to be back in a motel tonight," Kate said, slamming the tailgate closed a few minutes later.

Ty nodded. He looked off into the distance, smirking, wondering exactly what that final near-death experience had done to the walls Kate had erected between them.

"What's on your menu?" she asked, grinning.

He turned to face her, keeping his words more tender than flirtatious. "I've got a few things in mind." They climbed into either side of the cab.

"I can't wait to see what you order. It'll be my treat," Kate said. "Thanks for saving me," she added suddenly, voice soft. Ty wondered if she felt it, too—this harsh pang in the chest, half regret, half relief.

"You're the one who saved me," he said quietly, eyes

fixed in the distance. He heard Kate's nearly inaudible "whoa" as he did something he hadn't done in forever. He buckled his seat belt.

12

DINNER WAS A QUIET AFFAIR. After leaving the truck at the motor court the pair had walked to the bar, where Ty ate two steaks and two baked potatoes and Kate made calls to secure them a flight back to Los Angeles the next afternoon. They'd thoroughly missed their original booking.

Kate flipped her phone closed and Ty lifted his glass of beer to propose a toast.

"What's this to?" she asked, raising her own drink.

"To evolution," he said after thinking about it a moment. *To me finally finding my balls after a lifetime of faking it.*

Kate shrugged her agreement and they clinked their glasses. "Evolution."

"Do you remember much of what I said to you while I was carrying you to the safety crew?" Ty asked.

"No, not a word."

He shrugged. "No matter."

"Did I miss something good?"

"Nah. Just the ramblings of a very tired man." He was grateful she wouldn't remember all the promises he'd made when he'd been desperately bargaining for her to come out of the accident unharmed. There was one in particular that he wasn't prepared to make good on…letting her back on the location filming. Not only was that still out of the question, Ty had made a decision about the entire show, one that could only look ugly at the outset. But he'd decided. This was the way to go, and he wouldn't be dissuaded. He just needed time to get the network on board, and he needed Kate out of the picture if negotiations were to go the way he hoped. She'd never agree to the idea if he explained it up front, but if the pieces came together as he hoped, Ty thought he stood a fair chance of winning her over.

"I owe you Lakers tickets," she said, bringing him back to the present. "You found the safety crew first." Her tone was warm, her smile a bit wicked—both indicators of Ty's good chances once they got back to the motel.

"I look forward to collecting on that." He grinned guiltily to himself. Time would tell if she'd forgive him enough to make good on the promise before the NBA season wrapped.

They drained their glasses and walked along the dark street to the motel, and Ty's priorities shifted as if a switch had flipped from business to pleasure. He didn't bother going to his own room. As soon as Kate shut the door behind them he pulled her into his arms.

He felt her hugging back, not to the bone-crushing degree he was, but strong again. "You gave me such a scare this morning, Katie."

Her voice was stilted from the hug. "Now you know how I feel, each and every day."

"Goddamn...I don't know how you do it," he said, reliving for a moment just how terrified he'd been.

Kate slid out of the embrace and looked him in the eyes. "It's just how you are, Ty. I can't stop you from needing to do those things. Plus you make it look fun, all that death-defiance."

"Well, not anymore. I'm crossing over to the lame side

from now on—seat belts, harnesses, walk signs, all that boring old sensible crap."

She smiled. "I'll believe that when I see it…but good. I hope you do." She glanced around the room, probably feeling how Ty did, as though they'd just boarded an alien spacecraft. "You want to take a shower?" she asked, lips twitching, and exhausted or not, Ty's body responded in the unmistakable affirmative.

He followed her into the bathroom. While she brushed her teeth he warmed the water up to her preferred, scalding temperature.

Kate spit and asked, "Does all this feel really weird to you? You know…us? Like this. Finally lovers?"

He shook his head. "I've been imagining us this way for almost three years now. Everything seems just about right, finally."

With another smirk she began to undress him, her small fingers taking their time with his shirt snaps. Even with sleep-deprived circles beneath her eyes and an assortment of fresh scrapes and bruises, Ty didn't think she'd ever looked this beautiful. She finished undressing him and he returned the favor, savoring every inch of skin he exposed.

The hot water pummeled them as they entered the shower, steam and soap and shampoo reminding Ty that he was still a human being. He felt everything that ever stood between them being washed away, rinsed down the drain. Perhaps it was the exhaustion's doing, but he felt more raw and vulnerable than he ever had before in his life, here, naked under the bright bathroom lights, this close to Kate. It felt pretty bloody good.

Kate rinsed her hair with an indulgent sigh. With the requisites of hygiene met, she put her hands on Ty's sides, breaking into a smile he didn't recognize, one that averted her eyes and made the steam-flushed apples of her cheeks blush even deeper.

"Why are you smiling?"

"I'm finally going to get to have sex with you in a tacky motel room," she said, grin deepening. "My number one fantasy," she added in a scandalous whisper, holding up her index finger. She grabbed the soap from the tub's shelf and lathered her hands and slid them down his body, palms making a slippery assessment. Her fingers wrapped around him and Ty felt himself surrender, not only to the pleasure but to her, in every sense of the word. He closed his eyes, lost in the sensations, letting the moans rise out of his lungs, giving in completely. Her slick hands touched and fondled and teased until his arousal demanded more.

His eyes opened to find her still smiling up at him. "Take me to your bed, Miss Somersby."

THEY ABANDONED THE SHOWER and Kate toweled off, Ty lingering to shave. As she left the steamy bathroom, she noted with a frown that, predictably, all the sheets and covers had been replaced and the bed remade in their absence. She untucked everything at once. This had to be just like her fantasy, and that meant rumpled bedclothes. Ty climbed in beside her a few minutes later, smelling like lust and shaving cream, his naked body still slightly damp.

"What do you need, Katie?" he asked. Not waiting for an answer, his fingers were on her within seconds, stroking gently between her legs, making her want to open herself to him—not just her sex, but everything. All of her. The armor that Ty had accused her of hiding inside—it was sitting in the snow next to that trap now, rusting.

"I need to be with you," she whispered, meaning so much more than just this encounter. The sexual desire she'd been bubbling with a few minutes earlier had been eclipsed by something more elemental.

"I want that, too," he mumbled.

His touch made her dizzy, draining away any last vestiges of her old determination to keep her body and her spirit separate. She pulled away, sitting up and looking him over again. She couldn't get enough of this man. Her fingers trembled as she brushed them across his thighs. She felt a little frightened by the intensity of her emotions, but it was a fear she wanted to explore. When he tried to rise and do the same to her she pushed him back down with a firm hand.

"Let me enjoy you."

Ty allowed her hands to roam as they pleased, her palms, fingertips and nails surveying his bare body as he watched. She took in this man lying beneath her, more beautiful and strong and powerful than any she'd ever dreamed she'd be able to call her own, even for just one evening. She inventoried every inch of skin she'd lain awake fantasizing about, every inch she'd tended to when he'd been hurt.

In the end it was his mouth she wanted most. She lay down alongside him, their chests pressing as they melted into one another. Kate's fingers tangled in Ty's hair as she held his face to hers, tasting him, kissing him, her tongue discovering all the nuances of his mouth. Her fingertips memorized his face. He seemed to sense her wish, holding back his own explorations so that this caress could be hers to give.

She drew her lips away from his, gazing down at him.

"Tell me what you want."

"I want to…I want to see you. I want to have you, without you trying to prove something. I want the Ty who crawls into my bed at 3:00 am."

He shifted a little, seeming uncomfortable but game. "Okay."

"I want the Ty who no one else gets to see. Show me that." She smiled. "Even if it means the sex is lousy. Just show me what you wanted all those nights."

He nodded. "All right."

"Bearing in mind we don't have any condoms."

Ty's lips twitched but he didn't reply. He guided her to sitting and his hands surveyed her in return, tender, as though this were the first time they'd been undressed together. His touch was far different than the commanding variety he'd shown her in the woods. He seemed unsure of himself, his palms cupping her breasts cautiously, as if he feared he might hurt her, his mouth half-open with awe. He leaned in to suckle her, his lips gentle but needy. He moved to sit cross-legged and coaxed her into his lap, wrapping her legs around his waist, mindful of her sore ankle. His cock was hard and heavy, resting against her belly. Ty seemed unaware of it. His eyes were trained on her face as he kissed her, his mouth taking hers in quick, anxious tastes. Hands returning to her breasts, his fingers strummed her nipples, gently pinching, and she felt desire burning there as surely as she'd ever felt it between her legs.

She uttered his name against his mouth, like a sigh of sweet surrender. "What were you looking for, all those nights when you came to my bed?"

His palms left her breasts to stroke her neck, cup her jaw. "I didn't want to be alone with myself."

"Why does that scare you?"

He smiled, looking down. "You've seen me at my worst. Would you want to be trapped alone with that?"

"I like you at your worst."

"Maybe that's why I kept crawling into your bed, then. Because you can handle me. Maybe I want to be handled."

"Maybe. I like that side of you," she said. "The one you

don't show the cameras. I want the you that's human, the one nobody else gets…. Show me what that man wants."

"I'll try."

Kate rocked her hips back and Ty reached down to guide himself inside her, pulling her close again. He sealed their bodies together and she felt him, like a part of herself, pulsing in her core. He closed his eyes for a long moment, not moving, brow knitting.

"Oh God, Kate."

"What?" She stroked his face, wanting to understand what was going on inside that private mind.

He wrapped his arms tight around her, pulling her even closer, burying his mouth and nose in the hollow of her collarbone. A long exhalation steamed against her skin.

"This is it," he said finally, the words muffled.

"This is what?"

"This is what I wanted all those nights."

"And what is 'this'?"

"Just…this. Being inside you. Having you all around me. All your smells, and the way you feel. Your hands on me. I wanted you like this, letting me in, without it being about what I could give."

"Without any agendas?"

"Without any…anything. The only times I can ever just *be* are when you let me lie next to you. When it's just me, being a wreck, and you allowing me to be that way." He pushed his face harder against her, arms tightening. He held her in that position for a long time.

"You know what the hardest part of my job is?" Kate asked, not pausing for a reply. "It's the editing. It's watching as they take all the unscripted bits of you, between the segments, and get rid of them. Stripping it all away so only the version of you that you want the world to see is left. I wish everyone could see who you really are. You're so wonderful." The words surprised her even as they came out of her mouth. It was possibly the nicest and most sincere thing she'd ever said to him. To anyone.

"I don't want everyone to see that," he mumbled. "I only want you to."

They were quiet for a few minutes, and Kate let her body dissolve into their greater whole. Almost without meaning to she began, slowly at first, to rock with him, the motion intensifying until their hips were writhing, until she could feel the friction, feel him moving in and out of her.

Ty moaned, long and low, close to her ear, and the raw sound raised all the tiny hairs along her back. He transformed before her, the sensuality melting into raw sexuality, melting *her*. How had she ever lived without this?

They rocked together, feeding each other's excitement, in no rush for this exploration to reach a conclusion. Ty maneuvered her onto her back, taking control of their motions, thrilling her with that sensation of tender dominance as his large, powerful body commanded her and served her simultaneously.

"I want to taste you, Katie," he murmured.

"You can have anything you want."

After a dozen more beats he withdrew to stand before the bed. He pulled her by the calves to the edge of the mattress and knelt in front of her as she'd done for him in the little cabin. Kate glanced at the wall behind him, at the full-length mirror next to the bureau that revealed the entire scene to her—the long, elegant back muscles of the beautiful man before her. He coaxed her thighs open, eyes fixed on her center. He brought his face in close and she heard his deep inhalation.

"Sweet Christ, you smell amazing."

Kate responded with a firm hand on the back of his head, drawing him closer still. It had been a long time since she'd been treated to this particular intimacy, and even longer since she'd had a thoroughly impressive experience. Now she was itchy with impatience, sensing in every fiber of her being that this man would know exactly what her body wanted, instinctively.

Against her sensitive skin, Ty's breath flared, scorching hot. His eyes were half-lidded, the fingertips against her inner thighs unsteady. He made a soft noise, some affirmation or other, and gave her the softest graze of his lower lip. The subtle sensation raced like wildfire through her entire body.

"God, Ty."

He gave her a little more. His lips again, warm and rough, then a tiny sampling of the very tip of his tongue. Her fingers tangled tighter in his wet hair and he went further, bathing her clit with sensual licks, teasing it with kisses, diving in to sweep his tongue deeper, tasting her fully. The sounds that rose out of him stoked her fire as he slipped one finger, then two, inside her. She bucked against him and it only spurred him on.

He found what she liked with ease, his two hooked fingers playing inside against that magic, hidden spot, as his tongue flicked her clit with light, rapid, torturous licks. Her own noises began to drown out his.

In the mirror Kate watched his toned hips and ass shifting in tandem with the motion of his fingers. His body's eagerness, its *readiness,* thrilled her. The thought of him taking her again pulled hard on the proverbial trigger and all at once, she was gone, consciousness left behind as she was set adrift in pleasure. Ty moaned along with her as the shock waves radiated from deep inside. His mouth replaced his fingers, drinking in everything she gave him and whimpering with excitement.

He gave her a handful of seconds to recover before he

stood, angled his hard, swollen cock to her entrance and took her.

"Kate." He groaned, bracing his large hands on her hip bones and beginning to pump. He stopped. "Bugger. Be right back."

Kate waited, perplexed. He stepped to the jeans he'd ditched in the bathroom doorway and came back with a condom.

She laughed. "Been holding out on me, huh? Where on earth did you find that?"

He stood between her spread legs and equipped himself. "Bar restroom," he said with a smile. "Never doubt for a second about how classy I am, sweetheart."

"That's very thoughtful."

"You wish," he said, gliding back into her and picking up his refrain. "This is for me. So I can finally come inside you." He transformed before her, turning rough and aggressive, setting her on fire as always. She lay back so his body loomed above her, long and sleek and shining with sweat, every muscle she'd ever fantasized laboring for their mutual pleasure.

"Give me one more," he said between grunting breaths, nodding down between them. Kate ran an obedient hand down her belly to touch herself.

"Let me feel you come one more time before I have my turn," he moaned.

Ty had her body so primed and excited that it didn't even take a minute before she began to tighten around him like a fist, then he too let go. Chasing her climax, his hips hammered hard, slapping her thighs. His entire body tensed then froze, his abdomen tightening to signal his release.

Once he caught his breath, Ty disposed of the condom and tumbled into bed, gathering Kate into his strong arms, burying his face in her hair. For the first time ever, they both slept. Deep, dreamless, effortless sleep.

THE TRIP BACK SOUTH the next morning passed by in a blur. Kate was only vaguely aware of the snowy landscape whizzing by the truck, of the music and ads droning from the nondescript radio stations along the route. She let Ty drive the entire way as she drifted in and out of sleep.

Her head snapped up as the truck door slammed shut. She looked over to find he'd just climbed back into the cab. Outside were all the trappings of a proper town center, looking alien after the time they'd spent in the wilderness.

"Where are we?"

"Prince Albert."

"Already? Damn. Why'd we stop?"

"I had to swing by the post office. And I brought you a coffee." He slid a paper take-out cup into the holder on her side.

"Thanks."

"Where to next, PA?"

Kate smiled at the reintroduction of her title and dug the directions out of the glove box. She'd suspected—no, she'd *felt*—the night before, with all the intimacy they'd shared, that Ty was going to relent on his threats to take her job away. There was a certain delicacy to their new status as lovers, however. She decided not to bring up the topic until they were back in L.A., maybe after she'd worked on the editing for the final episode. Once their old routines were firmly reestablished. Perhaps by then Ty's decision would look as rash and reactionary to him as it did to her.

In what felt like no time they were aboard their flight to Denver, then on to Los Angeles.

Kate stepped out into the terminal and was flooded with a powerful emotion, akin to relief though not quite synonymous. A kind of exhausted euphoria, a thrill to be back among the mundane. It felt like a new beginning, and at the same time a return to the ordinary. Perhaps a return to the extraordinary, with her job still intact and, she hoped, a fantastic lover to round out the picture. Maybe they'd finally filled in the last blank that had always prevented Ty from being her definitive *everything*. That she even caught herself thinking in such terms nearly made her laugh out loud. Only a week ago these romantic thoughts would have struck her as patently *un*-Kate.

Beside her in the arrival lounge, Ty seemed cheerful but quiet, almost Zen-like compared to his usual frenetic baseline. Kate, conversely, found herself chattering in a voice so bright and optimistic it didn't register as her own.

"It's just so weird to be back, isn't it?" she said for about the third time in ten minutes, glancing around LAX with all the wonder of a child embarking on her first plane trip. "I can't wait to change my frigging clothes and take a walk on the beach. God, and get some real groceries and cook for a change. Although I'm so wound up now maybe I'll just order in and be a lazy bum all night."

They neared the baggage claim and Ty interrupted Kate's ramblings to offer a polite wave and a charming smile to a gawking young woman who clearly recognized him. Kate was glad the girl seemed content with mere acknowledgment. Good mood or no, she was sick to death of accepting proffered cameras and snapping photos of Ty with his arm around starry-eyed strangers.

"Ooh, that's mine." She pointed and Ty reached out to grab her frame pack from the carousel. The camera equipment came next in its protective black cases and she pulled everything off to one side to check for damage while Ty waited for his luggage.

"Wow, nothing's been lost. That must be a first," he said,

bags in hand, joining Kate as she made her inventory. An unwelcome jolt jarred her stomach as she discovered there was, in fact, something missing—something so important that her throat tightened with fear.

"Ty."

"Yeah?"

"The film isn't in here." She triple-checked the pockets in the case where the little memory cards should have been—where she'd put them *herself* before they'd left the motel.

"Really?" Ty asked.

"Really." She peeked in the cameras' slots and found those empty, as well. She glanced up at him, panicked. "Oh my God."

"Do you think someone stole them?" he asked, frowning.

"Why would someone take our footage but not the cameras?"

"They must think there's something highly valuable on them, then." Ty abandoned his frowning, one side of his mouth curling in a crooked, self-satisfied grin.

"Don't joke about—" Oh God, she'd forgotten. She hadn't only lost all the footage for the show, but the goddamn *sex video,* as well. "Holy crap! We're screwed. Why are you smiling?"

Ty's grin deepened and there was wickedness in it. Dripping from it. Kate nearly fell over with the breath she released.

"Oh my *God*, that was the worst joke ever. Don't *ever* scare me like that again." Her heart pounded against her ribs.

He chuckled. "Brilliant."

"Yeah, right. I thought we'd lost the whole episode there. And the… Anyway. Hand them over." She lowered her voice. "I need to edit out the dirty bits before we can send those to the editors."

"About that," Ty said.

"What?"

"I'm going to need to hang on to those, actually."

Kate's brows knitted. "Pardon me?"

"Sorry about the change in plans."

"Ty—"

"Don't worry," he said. "I'll get them to editorial, minus the sex. Your precious show will go on."

"We agreed that those would be mine, Ty."

"Don't be mad, Katie. It's just that I need some of what's on there, too." He smiled again, and when the teasing didn't stop Kate felt anger seep over her like lava.

"You said you trusted me."

"Oh, I do. But maybe you shouldn't have trusted *me*." His eyes glittered and he was smirking so thoroughly that his dimple appeared.

Kate felt her eyes widen with disbelief. "You *asshole*."

Ty smiled deeper, clearly pleased with himself. "I promise you'll understand soon enough."

"I think I understand just fine already." She seethed for a moment, then lunged for his bag. He relinquished it without protest and she knew after a few seconds of tearing through the contents that the cards weren't there. She glared up at him. "Where are they?"

"I posted them to myself, back in Prince Albert. To the network."

"I can get them just as easily as you can, then. I have just as much right to that film as you do."

"No, you don't."

"Yes, I do, I—"

"No, you don't," Ty repeated. "You're fired."

Kate's jaw dropped. She found herself able only to

blink for a few moments as her entire world fell down around her.

Ty smiled again, sadder this time. "Sorry. But it's not going to work out, Kate. I just can't do the show the way we have been anymore. I promise you'll understand in time—" He stopped, silenced by the hardest slap Kate had ever laid on a person. She hit him so hard it rang out like a sound effect, so hard his lip split, a tiny tickle of blood streaking his chin when he turned to face her. A dozen or more passersby stopped to stare, and Kate heard Ty's name muttered under strangers' breaths.

"I'm sorry." He almost looked sorry. Almost.

Kate wanted out. Now. The looming open space of the airport was going to crush her. Horrified and humiliated, she scanned Ty's unreadable face for a few seconds. She grabbed her pack, shouldered it and marched straight for the taxi stand without once looking back.

13

WINE SLOSHED FROM THE BOTTLE into the glass tumbler Kate had placed on the counter. No need for stemware. This wasn't celebration wine. This was six-dollar utility shiraz, exactly what the occasion called for. Disappointing, headache-inducing…Australian.

The bottle came with her into her bedroom—its contents stood little chance of surviving the evening and she might as well save herself several trips back to the kitchen. She and her glass settled down on the front edge of the bed and she clicked the TV on, flipping it to her former favorite channel. She commenced to fidget, waiting for the commercials to wrap and that familiar theme music to start up.

Kate had done this every Tuesday night for the three weeks she'd been back. *Survive This!* had a very fast production turnaround and most of the third season had aired while they'd still been filming the last few locations. Tonight was the finale, and this episode was different. Kate had had no input in the editing, for one thing, and more than that, this was their last trip together. The trip that had ended it all for her.

She took a fortifying breath. She could do this. She'd sit through an hour of this farce, watching Dom Tyler survive the Saskatchewan bush, trying her damnedest not to think of all the things that wouldn't have made the final cut—chiefly, hours of off-screen bickering and flirtation and the best, most meaningful sex of her life. The editing team might all be young, fresh-out-of-college hipsters, but Kate trusted them to do a decent job on the finished episode without her input. She just prayed they didn't all have copies of her sex video now. Those used to be her drinking buddies, for crying out loud. Awesome... How long now until she found herself on YouTube?

Nearly a month had passed since she'd seen Ty or spoken to him, even longer since she'd been by the offices of their production company. Two days after they'd landed in L.A., a courier had arrived on Kate's doorstep with all of her things from the *Survive This!* office. They'd been carefully packed and accompanied by a note in Ty's abysmal handwriting that read, "No hard feelings, I hope. Don't miss the season finale!" Days later she'd received the first severance check resulting from the "involuntary termination" of her job as his PA.

Several times he'd left her phone messages and emails, all of them upbeat and saying basically the same thing—he was sorry, he'd make this up to her, don't miss the show. She hadn't replied to a single one. And not once in all that time had Kate made any effort to start looking for another assistant job. She wasn't even sure it was what she wanted anymore, and frankly, she was overqualified now. Plus her heart was broken—her spirit, as well—and damn it, she was going to wallow. She'd claw her way into another entertainment job soon, maybe in production. Eventually. No, tomorrow. When the closing credits rolled tonight it would mark the official end of her self-indulgent mourning period.

A commercial for furniture polish ended just as the glowing digits on Kate's alarm clock ticked over to 8:00 p.m.

Her heart pounded, sabotaging all her attempts to convince herself she didn't care about this episode.

She held her breath. She waited for the first percussive thumps of the dramatic opening-credit music.

It didn't come.

She squinted at the screen, scrunching her brow in confusion at the scene.... Outdoors, the edge of a snowy woods on one side, a river on the other. The faint sound of a woman's voice, shouting.

Disembodied, Ty's voice spoke in hushed, documentarian tones from behind the camera.

"Did you hear that? That was definitely a call."

Kate watched herself round the bend, trudging through the slushy snow with a camera strapped around her front.

"Yes—it's an adult female, and I think she's spotted us. I'm just going to remain motionless, and hopefully I won't provoke an attack." Kate-on-screen neared. "This is just one of the many dangers that you put yourself down for when you enter the natural habitat of the Kate Somersby. We can see from her stance that this approach is one of postured aggression, though the look in the female's eye suggests that mating may be on her mind. Let's wait and see what she's after—" On screen, Kate reached the foreground and the bottom of her boot came up and disappeared below the lens's periphery. The camera and its operator toppled over backward and the shot went up into the sky and treetops.

Real-life Kate gawked.

The scene changed to footage of Kate looking up from where she sat on a boulder in a desert, perusing a wild edibles field guide. It was their trip to Nevada. Ty's voice came from behind the unsteady camera he was filming her with.

"Kate?" The voice paused. "Kate? Katie? Miss Somersby? Personal Assistant, I need you to personally assist me."

Kate remembered that. Ty had been winding her up the entire morning on purpose. He got that way when they'd been out on location for more than a couple of days, like an overtired child.

"Katie? What are you doing? Kate? Katie?"

The Kate on-screen glared up with a supremely irritated face. "What?"

"Can I autograph anything for you?"

She shook her head to express her supreme lack of amusement.

"What are you reading about, Katie? Share your wisdom with the viewers at home." The shaky camera zoomed in on her face as she looked up again.

"I'm trying to ascertain the most effective mushroom for putting one of us out of *your* misery, Ty."

"Poison, eh? That reminds me of a cracking song off that Bell Biv DeVoe album we listened to on the Yucatan. Sing it with me now, Kate." He began to sing the beginning of the track.

Finally, on-screen Kate smiled. "You are the most insufferable man on the planet."

The screen froze on Kate grinning in disbelief, against her better judgment. Ty's postproduction voice-over started up.

"This week we're bringing you a very special episode of *Survive This!* I'm Dom Tyler, and I'm going to share with you some invaluable tips and techniques for surviving in one of the harshest environments on the planet—my company. Because behind every jackass, there's a great woman.

"Kate Somersby here is the foremost expert in the world in this field." Footage of Kate sharpening an intimidatingly long hunting knife by a fire. Wading knee-deep in the

Amazon, clutching a wooden spear they'd been taught to fashion by a cooperative native tribe, ready to strike. Kate, rendered green and gray by the night-vision setting of the camera, half-awake in a sleeping bag in a tiny tent they'd shared during an overnight trip in British Columbia.

"You're creepy," on-screen Kate said to the camera with a yawn before turning over and going back to sleep.

Real-life Kate, perched on the end of her bed, felt her heart knocking wildly against her ribs. What on earth was this about? Why was she on television?

Ty's voice went on. "It was decided very recently that this show is not going to be returning for another season."

Kate's body gave a little jump of surprise and horror.

"But I couldn't let it end without showing everybody who is the real brains and brawn behind *Survive This!* It's this woman, right here. Kate is my entire off-camera, on-location crew. My assistant, camerawoman, associate film editor, researcher, occasional driver, PR agent, nurse, stylist, therapist, babysitter and partner, in just about every sense of the word...."

The entire hour-long show was promising to be like this—clips of Kate doing all the things she did behind the scenes. Catching food, assembling camera equipment, hauling water and frame packs and firewood, cocking a rifle... Kate looking dazed in a chair beside one of their regular film editors back in L.A., bleary-eyed at about 4:00 a.m. after hours of feverish digital postproduction work.

"How's your carrion coming along, Ty?" Kate's recorded voice asked when the scene changed again, and she remembered that night in Alaska like it was yesterday. No food except for a questionable half of a fish they'd found abandoned by an eagle or hawk, which the shot showed Ty cooking over a fire. Looking like a ragged mess, he glanced up, aiming a dryly cocked eyebrow past the lens, and then leaned forward to swivel the camera on its tripod. He aimed it the opposite way, at the stump where Kate was seated in clean and cozy state-of-the-art hiking attire, eating puffy marshmallows out of a plastic bag. She waved. He wasn't always the brat.

Uncertain if she was mortified or delighted by all of this, Kate simply watched, her jaw hanging open. She could sue him. She'd never signed any release saying it was okay to broadcast footage of her performing Public Enemy songs. Certainly not in a shitty motel room, wearing pajama pants and a camisole while Ty held the camera and shouted "Bleep!" over all the swears they'd memorized when that tape had kept them entertained on the long, hot, un-air-conditioned drive from Arizona to Washington State the previous summer.

Off-screen Kate couldn't seem to find it in herself to be angry—she came off extremely well in this, brattiness notwithstanding. She laughed at the next scene, remembering the time they'd filmed on a tiny island off Costa Rica. The clip showed Ty close up, the camera held by his own hand, and he was a wreck—sunburned, thirsty, half-starved, sleep-deprived, ant-bitten...not to mention surrounded by open ocean on all sides.

"In the past two days, I have eaten three tiny, raw, disgusting crabs, and drunk a cup of my own distilled piss. I just want you editors to see what's on the other side of this equation." He panned the shot around to where Kate was perched on a folding chair she'd brought, looking tanned and content in a striped bikini, drinking water out of a plastic liter bottle. She pushed her sunglasses to the top of her head and smiled. In real life she smiled, too. She could wring his neck for this....

The buzz of her doorbell made Kate jump about six

inches off her mattress and slop wine across her knees and the carpet.

"Crap." She glanced around and the buzzer sounded again. She gave up, abandoning the glass on the nightstand and jogging to the front door.

She left the chain on, glaring into the hall. "I knew it would be you."

Ty grinned through the three-inch gap. "Anything good on the telly, Kate? Or are you too angry to watch the series finale?"

"I don't even know what to say to you right now…. For starters, you promised we'd never do a clip-show."

"I can't help but feel I've been disappointing you ever since we left Canada, so I came right over. Oh, and I brought Chinese." He held up a grease-stained bag to show her. "Crab rangoons. Your favorite."

"I could sue you, you know."

"I know. Feel free. But now you know why I needed all that footage, Kate. Anyhow, it's all yours now." He held up another paper bag, shook it so Kate could hear the rattle of plastic.

She buried her forehead in her palm.

"Come on, Kate." He tugged on the chain with his free pinky.

"Give me my job back, Dom Tyler, and I'll let you in."

"No can do. The show's kaput. I've killed it. But I've come with another offer. From the network."

Kate squinted at him, curious. "What do you mean? What sort of offer?"

"Let me in and I'll tell you."

With a roll of her eyes she disengaged the chain and let him pass.

"'Bout bloody time."

"I'm still in shock, I'll have you know. How long have

you been planning all of this?" she demanded, shutting the door behind him.

Ty took a seat on the arm of her couch. "Ever since we made it back to civilization. Our crack editors helped me pull the clips together, in place of the final episode. The network wasn't impressed by the last-minute change, but I got my way in the end."

She chewed her lip. "Why'd you do it?"

"Because you deserve to have everyone see how hard you work," he said. "You deserve more credit. And frankly, you deserve the embarrassment."

"They shouldn't have let you show that film on TV without my permission."

"Don't worry," he said with a dismissive wave. "I'm very good at forging your signature."

"Excuse me?"

"Like I said, feel free to sue me."

"God…whatever. So what's this about an offer?"

Ty wandered to the kitchen counter and opened the take-out bag, rummaging. "Damn, they forgot the duck sauce."

Kate gave him an exasperated shove on the shoulder. "What's the offer?!"

He looked at her again, face aglow with triumph. "Well, they were upset that I'm pulling out of the show."

"Of course they are. It's a terrible idea."

"But I have to tell you, it's different now," he said. "You've made it different."

"So give me my job back."

"No, Kate, not like that." He finally abandoned the food and steered her to the living room couch. He sat beside her and took her hands in his own. "It's different, because for the first time in my life, I can't see any good reason to keep risking my neck."

"Or mine," she shot back, but the words came out soft, shy in the face of his pointed sincerity.

"No, not yours, especially. But they've agreed to option eight episodes of a new show."

"How nice for you," she mumbled.

His thumbs rubbed her knuckles. "Nice for both of us, if you want it. They won't do it without you on board."

She blinked. "Me? Specifically?"

"Yeah. When they saw the final cut of the episode that aired tonight, they said, 'Why on earth hasn't she been on camera all along?'"

"I don't—"

"You have no idea how bloody cute you are, do you?" Ty asked, smiling, clearly relishing how uncomfortable the praise was making her. "They loved it, Kate. They're willing to let us shoot another program. Sort of an environmental-travelogue-type of show. Conservation's hot right now. The show won't be dangerous, and there'll be less snow, I promise."

Kate frowned. "That doesn't sound very exciting."

"You're a sharp one, I'll give you that. Okay, there's a bit of a catch. I think they're sort of seeing it like our show, crossed with *The Newlyweds* or something. They kept saying, 'that chemistry—that's what this network needs! Where have you been hiding this girl?'"

"Oh *God*."

"What do you say, Kate?"

"I dunno," she said. "This is all really sudden. And it's a weird idea. It's like…Mulder and Scully on *Gilligan's Island*."

"That sounds pretty good, actually."

"Ty."

He ran his palms over her shoulders. "It's simple. It's what we've been doing all along, except with less danger, and two jerks on camera instead of just the one. I mean, are there any PAs in this town who don't secretly wish they were the ones who were famous? And *you* actually deserve it. Think it over, Kate. You'd look great accepting an Emmy. You can wear some of your pointy death-shoes. Free designer crap, goody-bags… All that gaudy celebrity stuff you get so moist over."

She shook her head. "Why'd you let me think you were a complete a-hole for a month while you were hatching this ridiculous plan?"

He smiled, a bit shy if she wasn't mistaken. "Well, for one thing, you'd have never given me permission to produce that episode."

"No, definitely not."

"Plus I needed time to pitch the idea, and for that I needed you out of the picture, otherwise you'd have rushed in and bollocks'd it all up by telling them you weren't interested. And for another thing…well, I love pissing you off. And I knew you'd forgive me."

She cocked a brow at him. "Did you then?"

Ty nodded. "You do, right? Forgive me?"

Kate sighed. "Probably…but I don't have an answer yet, about this proposal."

"Fine. You hungry? Let's eat, for goodness' sake." They walked to the kitchen and Ty opened her fridge, pulling out a bottle. "You still keep my favorite beer stocked, eh? Been missing me much?"

"That six-pack's been in there since before we left for Canada."

He scowled playfully, and they gathered their food. They adjourned to Kate's bedroom in time to catch the last fifteen minutes of the hour-long show.

"So what do you think?" Ty demanded.

"Honestly…? I never knew I had such great shoulders," Kate replied, studying the woman on the screen.

"I told you you're hot."

"This is so embarrassing," she said, unable to hide a dopey smile. She watched an entire montage of herself giving Ty the finger for various—and unfailingly well-deserved—reasons, caught either by his camera or appearing as a blurry, disembodied digit floating up to obscure her own lens.

"If it's not to your liking there's something else we can watch," Ty said, wiping his fingers on a napkin. He nodded mischievously to the memory cards he'd brought, the bag containing them visible through the kitchen doorway.

"Oh I *know* you didn't come here thinking you actually stood a chance of getting laid, did you?" Kate asked, faking incredulity. Then she froze. "None of the editors saw, did they? They don't know?"

"Christ Almighty, woman, how evil do you think I am? I studied filmmaking. I know how to splice dirty bits out of footage. Of course they don't know." He paused. "I bet everyone assumes we're like that, though."

"Probably," she admitted. "Especially now." She glanced at the screen. For all intents and purposes, these clips from the past three seasons looked like the private, candid home movies of an extremely well-suited couple.

"Don't think I didn't keep copies of the good stuff for myself," Ty said.

Kate rolled her eyes at him.

"Damn, you're badass," he said, pointing at Kate-on-TV with his beer bottle. "I can't wait to see the bonus features," he added, wiggling his eyebrows and glancing from her to the bag and back again.

"Like you haven't watched that a hundred times in the past three weeks."

"I haven't," he said, wide-eyed and innocent.

"Yeah, right."

"No, really, I haven't. Don't get me wrong—I bloody wanted to. But like I said before, this is about us." He nudged her with his elbow. "Nothing's any good without you. You have no idea how damn hard it's been for me these last few weeks, not being able to see you. And needless to say, I've slept like crap…. Probably deserved it, too, putting you through this."

Kate paused, taking in his familiar smell, letting her energy shift and mingle with his. "Well, I wouldn't have waited for you if I'd had the outtakes," she said eventually.

"Oh no?"

She shook her head. "No chance in hell."

"Well, I guess it's clear which of us is the gentleman. So what do you reckon? Feel like a private screening? It might give you ideas."

"What sorts of ideas might you be referring to, Mr. Tyler?" she asked pointedly.

"Be my lover, Kate. Please. Be my partner again."

She sipped her wine, avoiding his eyes. "You make it sound so easy."

"We'll ask the oracle, then." He rummaged in the greasy bag on the floor for the fortune cookies, stripping off the squeaky cellophane wrappers and holding them out for Kate to pick one. Ty cracked his open first. "'Your longtime work colleague and erstwhile dynamite sex partner will find your charms irresistible. Lucky numbers six, twelve, nine and thirty-three.'"

"You cheat. What does it really say?"

After he finished chewing Ty read out, "'Industriousness is the golden key to your prosperity. And Kate Somersby is dying for a good—'" Kate punched him on the arm. "Ow. So what's yours say?"

"It says," Kate began, unfolding the slip. "'Industri-ousness is the golden key to your prosperity.' Oh man, a repeat."

"Boo, cheap. Those things don't mean anything any-way…unless it says something else. Anything that'll make you admit you secretly love me."

Kate sat up straight, taken aback. "Is that what you want to hear?"

"If it was true…sure." Ty's face did a decent impres-sion of blasé flirtation, but his held breath and tight smile gave away just how much he had riding on her answer, emotionally.

"If it was true," she repeated. "You don't think it is?"

He shrugged. "That's what you told me, more or less, before we got back to civilization. That it was just physical. I know there's more to us, at least a *little* more, but I took you at your word, Kate. I've always trusted you."

She let her gaze fall to the carpet, wishing she could say the same. Wishing she'd listened to her heart before they'd parted so disastrously at LAX. Every fiber of her being had known inherently that this man was on her side, that he always had been. But she'd ignored all that and swallowed the lies her anger had fed her, all those incriminations that belonged to the people who'd hurt her so long ago.

Ty bumped her shoulder with his. "Don't look so glum. I brought one more bargaining chip with me." He left the bed to root through the paper bag on the counter. Expecting a digital sex tape, Kate wasn't surprised when he extracted a CD. She watched as he strode back into the bedroom and headed for the stereo beside the television, opened the changer and put the disc in.

"That's not a DVD player, pervert," she said.

"I know." Ty turned the TV off.

She frowned. "What are you up to?"

"I'm doing my damnedest to make you admit you love me." He hit Play on the CD player and adjusted the volume. The soft bass of an all-too-familiar song began to drift from the speakers, warming the room. Like magic, Kate was back at that cocktail party, two years ago.

"Dance with me?" Ty asked, as casually flirtatious as he'd been that night, murmuring those same words.

Shy, she shook her head, but she didn't resist when he pulled her to her feet and drew her into the steps, slow and lazy, meandering in circles, going nowhere. His hand was warm around hers, his other palm hot on her waist.

"I'm sorry I had to trick you," he mumbled against her temple. "I wanted to make everything right, and I needed time to work out the details. And I wanted to give you time, you know, to be cautious…about us."

He steered her back to the bed and manipulated their landing so she flopped onto his lap. "What do you say?"

"You said I could think it over."

"Not the show. Us. What about us?" He held her jaw in his hands and stared her down with kind, smiling eyes.

"Maybe… But you scare me, Ty. You move from woman to woman so frequently…I'm afraid to just be another one in the line."

He kissed her, slow and deliberate, softening her resistance. When he pulled away Kate felt as if she'd downed a very stiff drink.

"The women I dated… I kept moving on because none of them were you."

He cupped her chin and angled her face so she'd meet his eyes. "Please, Katie. We're so good together."

Kate held her breath and her tongue, held his gaze but did not reply.

He sighed and lowered his chin to her shoulder, his mouth

just below her ear. His words heated her skin. "You must know that I love you."

She swallowed and her whisper came out thick and quavery. "Do you?"

"Yeah. And I don't want you behind me anymore. I want you next to me, trudging through the woods or sleeping under the stars, or waking up in some hovel of a motel room."

"Or the back of a latex-stinking van," she muttered.

"Especially in the van," Ty confirmed.

"Is there a waiver I have to sign?"

Ty put his mouth to her neck again, kissed her skin. "Brat."

Kate grinned to herself. Ty kissed her again, his lips drifting down her throat to her collarbone and making her shiver. "What d'you say, Katie?"

Kate pushed him back by the shoulders and met his eyes. "I'm in."

His brow popped up. "Yeah?"

She nodded. "Yeah…I've missed you, the past few weeks. As pissed as I was—which was a lot—I missed you more." She cleared her throat, making the leap. "And I do love you."

His lips twitched. "You reckon?"

"Yeah. For I don't know how long." For a couple of breaths she held his eyes, and when the moment became too intense she dropped her gaze to his mouth. His lips looked smooth, no longer roughened by the cold air and harsh conditions of their final shoot.

She leaned in to kiss him and Kate could have sworn they were back in the woods again—the cold breeze, the scent of a wood fire, their scorching, shared heat. After a few moments she tore herself away to stare again into those eyes she knew so well.

Ty's mouth twitched into a grin so familiar it could have belonged to a childhood friend. And in a way, it did…the friend Kate had waited her whole life to find, someone who offered all the adventure and silliness she'd missed out on.

"So we're partners again?" she asked.

"We always have been."

She smiled. "It certainly feels that way."

"Good. Now I vote for dessert and bonus features."

Thinking of the film they had made together transported her in a breath, dragged her back three weeks and fifteen hundred miles to the shack, to the storm and the smell of wood smoke, Ty's strong, bare body in the firelight.

She pressed her nose to his throat and breathed him in, finding the elemental scent of his skin behind the civility of shaving cream. Whether he was filthy or clean, exhausted or rested, teasing or dead-serious, she loved this man.

"Maybe…but you know, since you fired me, I've sort of been missing the cameras…"

Ty affected a scandalized look. "Miss Somersby. Are you implying what I think you are?"

"I certainly hope so. Come on, Mr. Tyler. Let's go make a masterpiece."

Harlequin Blaze™

COMING NEXT MONTH

Available April 26, 2011

#609 DELICIOUS DO-OVER
Spring Break
Debbi Rawlins

#610 HIGH STAKES SEDUCTION
Uniformly Hot!
Lori Wilde

#611 JUST SURRENDER...
Harts of Texas
Kathleen O'Reilly

#612 JUST FOR THE NIGHT
24 Hours: Blackout
Tawny Weber

#613 TRUTH AND DARE
Candace Havens

#614 BREATHLESS DESCENT
Texas Hotzone
Lisa Renee Jones

You can find more information on upcoming
Harlequin® titles, free excerpts and more at
www.HarlequinInsideRomance.com.

REQUEST YOUR FREE BOOKS!
2 FREE NOVELS PLUS 2 FREE GIFTS!

red-hot reads!

YES! Please send me 2 FREE Harlequin® Blaze® novels and my 2 FREE gifts (gifts are worth about $10). After receiving them, if I don't wish to receive any more books, I can return the shipping statement marked "cancel." If I don't cancel, I will receive 6 brand-new novels every month and be billed just $4.24 per book in the U.S. or $4.71 per book in Canada. That's a saving of at least 15% off the cover price. It's quite a bargain. Shipping and handling is just 50¢ per book in the U.S. and 75¢ per book in Canada.* I understand that accepting the 2 free books and gifts places me under no obligation to buy anything. I can always return a shipment and cancel at any time. Even if I never buy another book, the two free books and gifts are mine to keep forever.

151/351 HDN FC4T

Name _____ (PLEASE PRINT) _____

Address _____ Apt. #

City _____ State/Prov. _____ Zip/Postal Code

Signature (if under 18, a parent or guardian must sign)

Mail to the **Reader Service:**
IN U.S.A.: P.O. Box 1867, Buffalo, NY 14240-1867
IN CANADA: P.O. Box 609, Fort Erie, Ontario L2A 5X3

Not valid for current subscribers to Harlequin Blaze books.

Want to try two free books from another line?
Call 1-800-873-8635 or visit www.ReaderService.com.

* Terms and prices subject to change without notice. Prices do not include applicable taxes. Sales tax applicable in N.Y. Canadian residents will be charged applicable taxes. Offer not valid in Quebec. This offer is limited to one order per household. All orders subject to credit approval. Credit or debit balances in a customer's account(s) may be offset by any other outstanding balance owed by or to the customer. Please allow 4 to 6 weeks for delivery. Offer available while quantities last.

Your Privacy—The Reader Service is committed to protecting your privacy. Our Privacy Policy is available online at www.ReaderService.com or upon request from the Reader Service.

We make a portion of our mailing list available to reputable third parties that offer products we believe may interest you. If you prefer that we not exchange your name with third parties, or if you wish to clarify or modify your communication preferences, please visit us at www.ReaderService.com/consumerchoice or write to us at Reader Service Preference Service, P.O. Box 9062, Buffalo, NY 14269. Include your complete name and address.

*With an evil force hell-bent on destruction,
two enemies must unite to find a truth that turns
all-too-personal when passions collide.*

*Enjoy a sneak peek in Jenna Kernan's next installment
in her original* TRACKER *series, GHOST STALKER,
available in May, only from Harlequin Nocturne.*

"**W**ho are you?" he snarled.

Jessie lifted her chin. "Your better."

His smile was cold. "Such arrogance could only come from a Niyanoka."

She nodded. "Why are you here?"

"I don't know." He glanced about her room. "I asked the birds to take me to a healer."

"And they have done so. Is that *all* you asked?"

"No. To lead them away from my friends." His eyes fluttered and she saw them roll over white.

Jessie straightened, preparing to flee, but he roused himself and mastered the momentary weakness. His eyes snapped open, locking on her.

Her heart hammered as she inched back.

"Lead who away?" she whispered, suddenly afraid of the answer.

"The ghosts. Nagi sent them to attack me so I would bring them to her."

The wolf must be deranged because Nagi did not send ghosts to attack living creatures. He captured the evil ones after their death if they refused to walk the Way of Souls, forcing them to face judgment.

"Her? The healer you seek is also female?"

"Michaela. She's Niyanoka, like you. The last Seer of Souls and Nagi wants her dead."

Jessie fell back to her seat on the carpet as the possibility of this ricocheted in her brain. Could it be true?

"Why should I believe you?" But she knew why. His black aura, the part that said he had been touched by death. Only a ghost could do that. But it made no sense.

Why would Nagi hunt one of her people and why would a Skinwalker want to protect her? She had been trained from birth to hate the Skinwalkers, to consider them a threat.

His intent blue eyes pinned her. Jessie felt her mouth go dry as she considered the impossible. Could the trickster be speaking the truth? Great Mystery, what evil was this?

She stared in astonishment. There was only one way to find her answers. But she had never even met a Skinwalker before and so did not even know if they dreamed.

But if he dreamed, she would have her chance to learn the truth.

Look for GHOST STALKER by Jenna Kernan,
available May only from Harlequin Nocturne,
wherever books and ebooks are sold.

Harlequin *Desire*

ALWAYS POWERFUL, PASSIONATE AND PROVOCATIVE.

USA TODAY BESTSELLING AUTHOR

MAUREEN CHILD

BRINGS YOU ANOTHER PASSIONATE TALE

KINGS *of* CALIFORNIA

KING'S MILLION-DOLLAR SECRET

Rafe King was labeled as the King who didn't know
how to love. And even he believed it. That is, until
the day he met Katie Charles. The one woman who
shows him taking chances in life can reap the best
rewards. Even when the odds are stacked against you.

Available May, wherever books are sold.

SD73096